Jude's look

A husky little so
in slow motion
her into his arms.

She took a shattered breath, thought about resisting, but clung to him instead, absorbing the unique male feel of him, glorying in the absolute rightness of his arms around her.

'Kellah…?' He lifted her chin, intending only to gauge her reaction. Instead, he found himself stirred beyond belief.

His breath rasped as he cupped her face, his thumbs ever so gently following the contours of her cheekbones. She looks so vulnerable, he thought, frowning down at the tiny flecks like gold dust in her eyes. And her skin—so soft, like velvet.

His chest rose as he breathed in deeply, capturing her fragrance—distinctive, special only to her. Oh, hell. He shook his head. He wasn't nearly ready for this…

Leah Martyn loves to create warm, believable characters for Medical Romance™. She is grounded firmly in rural Australia and the special qualities of the bush are reflected in her stories. For plots and possibilities, she bounces ideas off her husband on their early-morning walks. Browsing in bookshops and buying an armful of new releases is high on her list of enjoyable things to do.

DR CHRISTIE'S BRIDE

BY
LEAH MARTYN

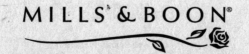

MILLS & BOON®

First published in Great Britain 2004
Harlequin Mills & Boon Limited,
Eton House, 18-24 Paradise Road, Richmond, Surrey TW9 1SR

© Leah Martyn 2004

ISBN 0 263 83924 9

Set in Times Roman 10½ on 12 pt.
03-0904-47181

Printed and bound in Spain
by Litografia Rosés, S.A., Barcelona

CHAPTER ONE

KELLAH would have given almost anything not to be having this conversation. But the last thing Bettina Remington needed was to sense her reluctance.

'I hope you don't mind me being so frank, Kellah.' Bettina crossed her arms, her fingers agitatedly pleating the sleeves of her stylish jacket.

'I'm your doctor, Bettina.' Kellah's gaze was full of compassion for the older woman. 'I'm sure I don't need to tell you anything you say to me will remain confidential.'

Bettina managed a tight little smile. 'Well, I didn't imagine you'd go running off to Leo.' She lifted her head, her gaze going to the brilliance of the morning sunshine outside the surgery window. When she looked back, her eyes had filled. 'Although perhaps someone should.'

'Hasn't your involvement with the support group helped at all?' In the awkward pause that followed, Kellah called on all her counselling skills, trying to distance herself from the fact that her patient was not only her friend but the wife of the senior partner as well.

'It was all right in its way, I suppose. But I couldn't seem to share my feelings.' Bettina gave a wobbly apologetic smile. 'I did try.'

'Please, Bettina, don't feel badly about it,' Kellah said gently. 'Groups aren't for everyone and resolving sensitive sexual issues after treatment for cancer is very personal.'

'But Leo's a doctor, for heaven's sake! *He* should be able to discuss things with me. I think if I'd lost a leg instead of having a breast removed, he'd have dealt with it better.'

Kellah's heart went out to her patient. But for the fact that after almost three years in the practice, she still found Leo Remington's rather reserved personality a bit daunting, she'd have broken the rules of patient confidentiality and gone to him herself. And somehow made him realise the absence of her husband's touch and sexual expression was lending a sharp edge to Bettina's fears and leaving her emotionally very lonely.

Instead, she tried to take on the role of mediator. 'It's been only a matter of months, Bettina. To some extent Leo is possibly still coming to grips with what's happened.'

Bettina was unimpressed. 'A little honest communication would go a long way. I just want him to hold me as if he means it, but he's treating me like I'm made of glass. If he can't stand the sight of me, why can't he just tell me?' She ran to a stop, biting her lips together painfully.

Oh, lord. Kellah sat up a little straighter, her jaw firming. If only she dared go to Leo and implore him to sort out this situation that was tying his wife in knots. But, of course, she couldn't...

'Heavens, look at the time!' Bettina ended the tense moment, blinking a jerky look at her watch. 'Thank you for seeing me at such short notice, Kellah. And so early. And really, I do know there aren't any magic formulas but it *has* helped to let all this angst out. You're such a calm person.'

Kellah smoothed back a stray tendril of dark hair and managed a wry smile. She rose to her feet to see her patient out. 'Honestly, Bettina, I think you should take heart from the fact that Leo has been the one to initiate this time away. Perhaps, like you, he's feeling you need some quality time as a couple, and what better way than taking a fabulous cruise around the South Pacific?'

'Put like that…' Thoughtfully, Bettina raised a hand, toying with the strand of tiny seed pearls at her throat. 'Actually, I've, um, bought some rather nice clothes for the holiday—including some wildly expensive silk lingerie,' she tacked on almost shyly.

'Good for you,' Kellah approved. 'And while you're away, keep up the vitamin E oil on your scar tissue. Remember, your body is still beautiful.'

'You've been such a good friend through this, Kellah.' Bettina swallowed uncomfortably. 'I can only hope and pray this time away with Leo will give us back some kind of normal life.'

In a spontaneous gesture, Kellah gave the older woman a warm hug. 'Just enjoy yourself. Oh—and send me a postcard.'

'Absolutely,' Bettina promised, fluttering a wave as she left, her demeanour seemingly marginally lighter than when she'd arrived.

Kellah closed the door of her consulting room softly and leaned against it for a moment. Being the confidante of so many of her patients weighed heavily. And sometimes she felt the need to lean on someone herself. A special someone.

Not that she was actively looking for that someone.

She shrugged away the niggling thought. Being single wasn't something that bothered her too much. But only yesterday her sister Jillian had been rabbiting on about the boring predictability of Kellah's life.

'You're thirty-one, Kel. Time's marching on. You hardly ever meet any men.'

'I meet men all the time,' Kellah had defended, absently smoothing the downy hair of her two-year-old niece, Gemma, who was snuggled contentedly on her aunt's lap.

'I meant *eligible* men.' Jillian clicked her tongue. 'You work appallingly long hours in that wretched surgery and then come home to an empty apartment. You need to make time for other things.'

'Like babysitting your kids?' Kellah raised well-shaped dark brows at her younger sister. 'Even though I love them to bits, I do give them quite a bit of this time you think I should be doing something with.'

'Honey, I realise that,' Jillian said earnestly. 'You've probably saved Will and me from going dotty. But you must know Matty and Gem adore spending time with you.'

Kellah's look was wry. 'That's because I'm like the fairy godmother while you're the regular mother.'

Jillian helped herself to another slice of banana bread. 'Uh, you're not still hung up on Scott, are you?'

Kellah made a click of annoyance. 'Where did that observation spring from? Scott was ages ago. He preferred someone else, that's all.'

Jilly sniffed. 'A lot of someone elses, if you ask me. He was a self-serving rat. And how dared he? You were worth ten of those—'

'Jilly, stop.' Kellah placed her hand on her sister's forearm. 'It's sweet of you to want to look out for me but I'd be unlucky to meet someone like Scott again,' she said, adding dryly, 'I'll be sure to look out for the signs—OK?'

Jilly made a face. 'As long as you recognise them

before you're through the gate and up the garden path again. Oh, by the way, are you working on Saturday?'

'Jilly, you're shameless.' Despite knowing she was being set up ever so nicely, Kellah had no option but to laugh. 'But to answer your question, I'm not on call. Leo's doing his last rota before he takes leave. Do I gather you want help with the children?'

'It's the fête at Matt's kindy and I kind of wanted to show the flag a bit. I'm on the committee.'

'And you can't be there?'

'I'm directing the new play for our Little Theatre and Saturday is the only day everyone can turn up for the rehearsal. By the way, I'll reserve you a couple of tickets. Ask someone nice to go along with you.'

Meaning a man. Kellah swept her gaze briefly to the ceiling. Her sister was about as subtle as a sledgehammer. 'Can't Will step in for you at the fête?'

'He's playing in some fours comp with his golf club. If someone drops out, the others get bent out of shape about it.'

'So in a nutshell, you want me to take Matthew and Gem to the fête?'

'If you wouldn't mind.' Jillian's big violet eyes softened pleadingly. 'I wouldn't ask but Matty is so excited about it. They're having a jumping castle and I've promised him a go on it. I've done my bit and made cakes and sweets. So if you'd deliver them to the various stalls with my apologies and then just give the kids an hour or so on the play equipment, it would be fantastic.'

So that's my Saturday taken care of. Kellah came back to the present with a snap. Glancing at her watch, she sighed and walked across to her desk, stooping to browse through some reports in her in-tray. Another long day loomed ahead and it was barely eight-thirty.

The smell of freshly brewed coffee permeated enticingly from the staffroom and her first patient wasn't due until nine. But something held Kellah back from joining the other members of the practice for their usual early cuppa and light-hearted social interaction.

That *something* was Jude Christie. He was the locum filling in for Leo, gradually taking over the senior doctor's list of patients.

Kellah didn't know what to make of him. She only knew everything about the man unsettled her. And she didn't like the feeling one little bit.

A second later, the rat-a-tat on her door had her looking up sharply. 'Come in,' she called, at the same time holding some paperwork against her chest in an almost defensive action.

Jude poked his head around the door. 'Ah, thought so.' Pushing the door open, he sauntered into the room, aiming an accusing finger at Kellah. 'I'm beginning to think you're some kind of workaholic, Dr Beaumont.'

'Good morning to you, too, Dr Christie,' Kellah said blandly. And as their gazes locked, the same tiny quiver of something unfamiliar curled around her throat and tightened.

'My, aren't we formal.' He jerked a thumb towards the open door. 'Come on, Doc. Coffee's up and I've been sent to fetch you.'

A reluctant smile pleated Kellah's mouth at the corners. 'Have you just?'

'Mmm.' Arms folded, he parked himself on the edge of her desk. 'Or I could get us both a cup and have it in here with you.'

Oh, heavens, not that! Kellah felt her pulse rocketing at the thought. 'No—no, I was about to join you all, anyway.'

'Good,' he said softly. 'Let's go, then.'

She watched, mesmerised, as he levered himself away from the desk and stood upright. Leaning across, he plucked the sheaf of papers from her nerveless fingers and dropped them back into the tray and she found herself trapped again by those extraordinary navy blue eyes.

I don't believe any of this. Kellah gathered her scattered thought processes, following meekly behind him, as they left her office. Confused, she found her gaze dropping from his broad shoulders and lingering over lean hips and long legs in faded denim that hugged his body intimately like a second skin, finally ending in frayed hems that brushed the tops of the well-worn trainers on his feet.

Surely he wasn't about to conduct his surgery dressed like that, she thought crossly in an effort to counteract the feeling of vulnerability Jude seemed to generate in her so easily.

And he was wearing a T-shirt, for heaven's sake, emblazoned with a message that was far from appropriate for a medical practice: SATISFACTION GUARANTEED. She made a silent *tsk* in her throat, unnerved all over again when her shoulder brushed against his upper arm as he stood back to allow her to enter the staffroom.

Their gazes swivelled and caught and Jude's eyes held hers for a long moment before he looked away, leaving her oddly shaken and more confused than ever.

'About time, you two!' Teri O'Brien, their receptionist, sprang to her feet and began pouring coffee into the cheerful red mugs.

Kellah took a breath to steady herself, then unobtrusively she selected one of the mugs of coffee and went to stand by the window.

'Hey, Theresa Jane.' Jude turned to Teri with a questioning look. 'You haven't scoffed all my muffins, have you?' Dark head bent, he poured a dollop of milk into his coffee.

'No, silly.' Teri gave a gurgling laugh. 'I nuked them and wrapped them in foil to keep warm. They're yummy by the way.'

'Of course. I'm a good cook,' he stated modestly. Locating the muffins, he unfurled the foil-wrapped parcel and proffered it to Kellah.

It should have been easy to reach out and take one of his muffins but she felt frozen to the spot, her fingers executing a white-knuckled grip on the handle of her coffee mug. 'Ah…no, thanks. I'm fine.'

'They're good,' he coaxed. 'Loaded with fresh peaches and roasted macadamia nuts.'

Kellah felt pushed into a corner, quite unable to deal with the ridiculous situation. Why on earth was she screwing herself into a knot over a damned muffin? She swallowed uncomfortably and when she glanced across at Jude, he had a look in his eyes that doubled her unease. It suddenly seemed easier to comply. 'OK, then. Thanks.'

'You're welcome.' He held her gaze for a moment longer than was comfortable, before he moved away and slid the plate back onto the table.

Trying to look relaxed and at ease, she placed her mug on the windowsill and took a bite of her muffin. It was mouth-wateringly crumbly and she tucked in, justifying a much-needed energy boost before she began her surgery. The conversation buzzed around her and she relaxed for a moment, watching the various personalities interact.

There was Teri, of course, bubbly, very good at her job on the reception desk. She couldn't be more than twenty, Kellah thought wryly, and yet she handled Jude's rather teasing manner with ease, giving back as much flippancy as he dished out.

Reflectively, Kellah took a mouthful of her coffee, knowing there was no way on earth she could cope so effortlessly around him.

Almost as if she were watching a play, her gaze switched to Sophie Mellor, the RN for the practice. Gathering up her curtain of ash-blonde hair, Sophie twisted it expertly into a knot on the nape of her elegant neck, asking, 'How's the column coming, Jude? Got a pen name yet?'

He grimaced. 'Nothing suitable apparently.'

Determined not be left out of the discussion, Teri plonked herself down opposite him and swung her long legs onto another of the high stools. She shot him a wicked little wink. 'What about Hop-along Casualty?'

His mouth quirked. 'Now, why didn't I think of that?'

'You're writing a column?' Kellah's question came out abruptly and she realised belatedly it had sounded almost accusing.

Turning his head, Jude looked right into her eyes. 'It's not AMJ material. Just a low-key medical advice section for the local free paper. My sister's the editor,' he off-loaded casually. 'Her usual columnist is off on extended leave, so Sarah asked me if I'd fill in.'

Presumably, Sarah was his sister, Kellah decided. Perhaps the man had hidden depths after all...

'Frankly, Jude, I hope you can manage something with a bit more substance than the present content.' Maggie McKee, the practice manager, had picked up the tail end of the conversation as she'd come into the staff-room. Wrinkling her nose in distaste, she waved away

Jude's offer of coffee, selecting one of her herbal teabags instead.

Jude, however, seemed unfazed. 'The information is supposed to be easily digestible.'

'What about keeping to a theme?' Against her better judgement, Kellah found herself being drawn into the discussion.

'Could work, I guess.' Jude gave a tiny nod of acknowledgment. 'As in different questions but slanted towards the same theme?'

'And a different theme each week.'

'I think you're onto something here, Doc.' Jude's brows came together in consideration. 'That's not bad. Let's hook up after work and expand on it. Your place or mine?'

Lord, the man was incorrigible. Kellah swallowed hard, imagining every eye was on her, every ear attuned for her reaction. Damn Jude Christie for putting her on the spot like this! 'I'll have to get back to you,' she waffled. 'I think I may have a consult after hours.'

Jude's look held faint scepticism. 'OK.' He lifted a shoulder dismissively. Sliding off his stool, he stretched. 'I'm off home to shower and change. I had a call-out at four this morning. Had to hospitalise one of Leo's patients with an asthma attack.'

Kellah swung round from washing her mug at the sink. 'Would that be Tallara Muir by any chance?'

'Yes.' A shadow came over his face and his mouth compressed. 'Poor little kid.' Jude shook his head, still hearing the youngster fighting for breath. 'She's only thirteen and apparently she's been in and out of hospital for most of her life.'

Kellah bit softly into her lower lip. 'I took her over when Leo was on leave several months back. I had the feeling then her mother was still smoking around her. But as usual Tally was totally loyal and noncommittal.'

Maggie clicked her tongue. 'I sometimes wonder who exactly *is* the mother in that household.'

'Lauren Muir is a sole supporting parent,' Kellah responded quietly. 'She works awful hours in that roadhouse. It can't be easy for either of them.'

Maggie shrugged expressively. 'I've no patience with people who say they can't quit smoking. I did it when I saw what it was doing to my insides.'

'Some folk find it very difficult, Maggie.' Jude was diplomatic. 'And it's the drug they cling to when they're constantly under stress.'

Suddenly, Kellah felt herself looking at Jude in a new light, somehow grateful he'd understood that nothing about delivering health care was ever clear-cut. 'So, what's Tally's prognosis at the moment?'

Jude ran his hands through his hair and locked them at the back of his neck. 'She was getting some relief from the nebuliser and, of course, she's on a drip. Perhaps we need to up her physio regime. Anyway, I'll pop in and see her after surgery. But I think I'd have heard if she wasn't settling.'

In the shower, Jude lathered himself, letting the warm jet of water spray over his head and slick down over his chest and shoulders to puddle around his feet. His decision to settle in Chadwick was going to work. He'd make it work. He was done with wandering around the world. Or running from life, as his sister had so cryptically put it.

He thought about Chadwick itself. As a sprawling rural Queensland town, it had plenty going for it. With its origins in coal mining and now diversified into wine growing and a dozen other industries, the place had a history as long as your arm. And if he felt like a change of scene, it was reasonably close to both Brisbane and the coast.

Turning off the shower, he slicked back his hair. Working as locum meant he was probably going to be out of a job once Leo came back, but he'd worry about that later. No doubt he could get a place at the local hospital. They were always on the lookout for experienced medical officers for the emergency department. His mouth drew in. These days he much preferred general practice but if he had no choice, so be it…

The fact was, whatever way he looked at it, a new chapter of his life was about to begin and he wasn't jaded enough not to find that part a professional challenge.

But what of the personal implications? Without him even trying, his thoughts flew to the only female MO in the practice.

Kellah Beaumont.

Even now his head was full of images of her. Her cloud of dark hair pulled back so neatly except for the wayward tendrils that brushed across her cheekbones. Her swan-like neck and straight little nose. And her mouth, wide and expressive. A mouth that looked like it should smile constantly and yet didn't. At least, not around him. And eyes dark brown and beautiful. Eyes to drown in. Hell, he was getting delusional.

He gave free rein to a wryly crooked smile, admitting so far he'd made only the slightest dent in the process of getting to know her. Personality-wise, the lady made self-containment an art form. But surely away from the practice she had a lighter side…

But was he ever going to get the chance to find out?

Suddenly, he felt a thread of alarm. Hell, don't even go there, Christie, he warned himself bleakly, squeezing his eyes shut.

Since Angie's death three years ago, he'd been virtually celibate. Not that he'd lacked offers of comfort after his loss. He'd accepted and then wished he hadn't. Oblivion had been fleeting and the residue of guilt that had followed had been so emotionally draining he'd kept himself very much to himself ever since.

With a muttered curse, he dragged on a pair of freshly laundered chinos and a light blue button-down shirt. Stuffing his feet into his favourite leather boots, he took off out to his car.

Thank heaven he could lose himself in his work. It was the only medium where he felt totally in control. Safe. Perhaps it was destined to always be that way...

CHAPTER TWO

KELLAH logged her last patient's details into the computer and breathed a sigh of relief. It had been the oddest kind of day and she was glad it was at an end.

Thankfully, she'd managed to avoid Jude for the whole day. But that couldn't go on indefinitely. She felt the warmth creep up her throat and grimaced. Nobody had ever got under her skin like that man did and after all that nonsense about the muffins in the staffroom this morning…

She shook her head as if to clear it. She had the weekend ahead to get herself back on an even keel. And she would. It was just a case of mind over matter.

A soft smile played around her mouth. It would be fun to spend tomorrow with Matthew and little Gemma. They were so lively, so full of energy but so sweet when they'd had their baths, settling down each side of her on the sofa while she read them a story.

Children of her own? The thought tugged at her heart-strings. Was Jilly right? she wondered broodingly. Perhaps. But to have children, she needed the right man and so far, despite her best efforts, he just hadn't come along.

Feeling strangely philosophical, she raised her arms and stretched and then pushed herself upright.

She'd call in at that new Italian place on the way home, and treat herself to a take-away. Perhaps veal scallopine and some of their delicious focaccia bread to accompany it. The food would go nicely with the Australian merlot she'd bought last weekend and hadn't yet opened...

'Ah, Kellah. Glad I caught you.' Dr Tony Spiteri, the third permanent member of the practice, poked his head around the door.

'Good heavens,' Kellah said dryly, and beckoned him in. 'Surely you weren't pining for the sight of the place? How was the conference?' Tony had been in Sydney for the past week and she hadn't expected him back until Monday.

He rocked his hand. 'I've been to better. The keynote speaker was a bit of a drag. Caught myself nodding off, I'm afraid.'

Kellah smothered a grin. She'd been there and done that. 'Something I can do for you, Tony?'

'Actually, I just wanted to run something past you.' He planted himself against the edge of her desk and folded his arms. 'Cassie and I wondered whether we should put on a farewell dinner for Leo and Bettina before they go on their cruise. He's finishing two weeks from today so we'd need to get weaving.'

'I'm not sure.' Kellah turned and collected her medical case from its locker. 'I spoke to Bettina this morning.'

'And?'

'I have the feeling she just wants to be away out of the place and on her holiday.'

'And Leo?' Idly Tony lifted one of the cassette tapes she'd left in her filing tray, studied the title for a second and slipped it back.

Kellah sighed audibly. 'Tony, I have no idea where Leo's head is at the moment.' *I just know he seems clueless about Bettina's present needs,* she tacked on silently.

Tony straightened away from her desk and sent her a grim little smile. 'You don't think they're heading for a divorce, do you?'

'Oh, surely not.' Kellah was appalled. 'They've been married for twenty years…'

Tony palmed a shrug. After a second he said, 'So you don't think a farewell dinner is a good idea?'

'Oh, lord, Tony.' Kellah shook her head. 'You've known Leo longer than I have. What does your gut feeling tell you?'

'He wouldn't thank us for the fuss.'

'There you are, then.'

'Knock, knock.' Jude's dark head zoomed in through the partially open door, his brows raised in query. 'Is this a private meeting or can the locum join in?'

Kellah's fingers tightened on the handle of her medical case as Tony stretched out a hand towards Jude.

'Sorry I haven't been around much to help you settle in, mate,' Tony apologised as the two shook hands briefly. 'How's it going?'

'Pretty well.' Jude's hands propped against his hips. 'Sure I'm not intruding?' His blue gaze flicked from one to the other.

Tony shook his head. 'Your timing couldn't be better. I'm off home to my family and Kellah is all squared away. It's Friday, folks.' His eyes twinkled behind his steel-rimmed spectacles. 'Why don't the pair of you relax over a drink somewhere?'

Kellah tensed. Thanks for nothing, Tony. As if she didn't have enough on her plate with Jilly and her determined matchmaking. Turning her head, she stared directly at Jude. For an endless moment their gazes locked until he gave an almost imperceptible lift of his shoulder.

So, how did she interpret that? Kellah wondered, confused. It was obvious no spontaneous invitation was going to be forthcoming from *him*.

'Ah… OK, then,' Tony said too heartily into the deepening pool of silence and made a show of loosening his tie. 'See you both on Monday.'

'You bet,' Jude called over his shoulder, as Tony made a hasty exit. 'Have a good weekend.'

A beat of silence.

'I've laid concrete with more finesse than that,' Jude muttered, his gaze swinging back to Kellah. But then he grinned, a lazy, wry grin that dissolved the flare of tension between them. 'I wondered whether you'd be free to come to the hospital with me?'

Kellah eyed him warily. 'In what capacity?'

'Oh, nothing too daunting. I want to check on Tallara Muir. You know the family, don't you?'

'Not well but—'

'But well enough for Tally to be more comfortable with you than me.'

'Perhaps.'

'Of course, if you've somewhere else you need to be…'

'No,' Kellah said too quickly, unnerved by the tap-dance of her heart against her ribs. What on earth did she think she was doing? Going anywhere with Jude Christie was madness. But if it was health-related… 'I've nothing planned.'

'Good. Thanks, Kellah.' He gave her a very sweet smile. 'I appreciate this.'

They left by the rear door of the practice, setting the alarm as they went.

'I imagine you'll want to take your own car.' Jude

stopped beside his metallic grey Audi. 'Meet you in the hospital foyer, OK?'

Kellah nodded and took the few paces to her own modest sedan.

In the children's unit, they found Tallara perched high against the pillows, her eyes following a popular teenage sit-com on the small television screen. At the doctors' approach, she turned from the screen, a look of resignation on her thin little face.

'Hi, Tallara.' Jude picked up the chart from the end of the bed. 'I've brought Dr Kellah along to see you.'

Kellah smiled at the youngster. 'What kind of day have you had, Tally?'

'OK…'

Which tells me precisely nothing, Kellah lamented, running her stethoscope over the child's chest and back.

'Can I go home?' Tally turned huge dark eyes hopefully on Kellah as she placed her stethoscope aside.

'Sorry, sweetheart.' Jude replaced the chart carefully. 'We need to get you stable again.'

Kellah dragged up a chair and lowered herself to the child's level. 'Honey, we know it's hard being in hospital and missing your friends at school.'

Tally's mouth wobbled. 'I hate all this stuff I have to do.'

'What stuff?' Jude asked gently, leaning forward, listening.

'Like this awful drip thing.' Tally held up her arm and grimaced. 'And the nebuliser and the Ventolin.' She stopped and swallowed jerkily. 'And everyone telling me to cough up and all the water I'm s'posed to drink…' She drew to a halt, tears welling suddenly in her eyes.

'Tally, we know it's no fun having asthma.' Kellah leaned forward and cupped her hand around the youngster's cheek. 'Has your mum been in today?'

Tally brightened and nodded. 'She spent a whole hour with me this afternoon. We did a crossword. It was fun. I love crossword puzzles.'

'Then you must be very clever.' Kellah smiled. 'I'm useless at them.'

'Me, too,' Jude chimed in with a wry grin at his young patient. 'I always end up going to the answers.'

Tally gave a muffled giggle and brushed the backs of her hands against her eyes. 'That's cheating. Mum says you have to read lots to be good at crosswords.'

'Ah, that's where I've gone wrong.' Jude caught Kellah's eye and smothered a grin. 'I can see I'll have to join the local library.'

'You could do a lot worse, Doctor.' Hiding a smile, Kellah got to her feet. 'We'll look in again in the morning, Tally.'

The youngster fingered the end of her long plait. 'Will I be able to go home?'

'Let's see what kind of night you have,' Jude came in gently. 'Now, have you something to read?'

The child nodded. 'Mum brought me in some library books.'

Kellah sensed Jude's preoccupation as they made their way back to the nurses' station. 'Perhaps we could have a chat to the reg about increasing the percussion on Tally's back,' she suggested.

'Mmm.' He scraped a hand around his jaw. 'We need to get that cough productive somehow. But regardless of what can be done here for Tally, I'm loath to send her back to the same home environment for the same thing to happen all over again in another month.'

'In that case, we'll have to speak to the mother,' Kellah said practically, unaware she'd already aligned herself with Jude in deciding to pursue a better quality of life for this youngster.

'You wouldn't mind?' Jude's eyebrows lifted sharply.

Kellah shrugged. 'We're all about healing, aren't we? I just can't understand why Leo has let Tally's situation drift on as long as this.' She stopped and looked a little shamefaced. 'Actually, that wasn't very kind. He's had a lot on his plate recently.'

'Bettina's cancer scare?'

Kellah nodded and bit her lip. 'But things are looking more hopeful in that direction now.' She kept her fingers firmly crossed.

A few minutes later, after a brief chat with the paediatric registrar, Hannah Gordon, the two medical officers made their way back to the lift.

'Do you have plans for the rest of the evening?' Jude's suddenly brooding gaze raked her face.

'No… I don't.' Kellah felt her heart flip. He stood so close, the pale linen of his shirt the only barrier between her eyes and the broad masculinity of his chest.

'No consult, then?'

She felt her face flame at the thought he'd obviously seen right through her pathetic excuse earlier. She swallowed uncomfortably. 'There was no consult.'

'I see…' Jude tilted his head, his gaze narrowing as he lifted a soft ringlet away from the side of her face. 'Then why don't we try to see Mrs Muir now?'

Kellah could hardly concentrate on his words, simply staring at him, unnerved by her body's instinctive response to his touch.

'It was just an idea.' Jude whipped his hand away, shoving it into his back pocket. Why on earth had he done that? *Touched* her. His jaw clenched and he noticed the way her gaze fluttered down. Hell! He'd only succeeded in totally embarrassing them both. 'Uh, I really don't want to wait on this.' His tone was suddenly businesslike as he tried to cover the awkward moment. 'Tally's mum has got to be brought to the realisation of just how tenuous her child's situation is.'

'Yes.' Kellah tried to concentrate. To forget the touch of his fingers against her skin. And all it implied. What he'd suggested made sense. Of course it did. And she should be relieved Jude was taking his responsibilities as locum so seriously.

The lift arrived and they got in. 'Lauren works at the roadhouse just outside the town proper,' Kellah informed him. 'She's the cook.'

'So one would think she gets a break some time during the course of her shift?' Jude surmised quietly.

Kellah looked up to find those haunting blue eyes studying her face. 'I imagine so.' Her tone was carefully neutral. 'But you can't go at this like a bull at a gate,' she cautioned.

'Point taken. But somehow I've got to get through to her.'

Dusk was falling when they made their way back to the car park. Kellah looked up at the sweep of clear sky and the early twinkling necklace of stars. 'Should we travel together?' Her arms tightened across the jacket she held in front of her.

'Probably false economy to take two cars,' Jude agreed, propping himself against the door of his Audi, his feet crossed at the ankles, accentuating the length of his legs and the leanness of his hips. 'We'll take mine and I'll drop you back here after we've seen Mrs Muir, if that's OK?'

'Fine.' Kellah moved quickly to the passenger side,

refusing to indulge herself in the doubtful pleasure of admiring him.

At the roadhouse they went across to the dining area and Jude asked for Lauren Muir.

'I'll just get her,' the obliging young waiter who was setting tables said easily. He disappeared through the swing doors to what was presumably the kitchen. 'Lauren!' he bellowed. 'Someone asking for you outside.'

'Takes me back.' Jude's tone was laced with dry humour.

Kellah blinked. 'In what way?'

He shot her a rueful grin. 'I worked as a kitchen hand while I was at uni.'

'How on earth did you find time to study?'

'I was young. It's amazing how one can survive with so little sleep.' He raised an eyebrow just slightly and queried, 'What about you? Did you have a part-time job through medical school?'

'No. My parents paid my fees.' Her small chin lifted as if in cool dismissal of further probing. 'Ah, here's Lauren now,' she said, as the young woman batted her way through the swing doors and stopped dead in her tracks.

Recognising the two doctors, Lauren's hand went to her heart. 'It's not Tally, is it?'

'She's doing OK, Lauren,' Kellah reassured hastily, seeing the look of alarm on the mother's face.

'But she's not stabilising as well as we'd hoped, Mrs Muir,' Jude came in with quiet authority. 'And as Dr Beaumont has treated Tally before, I've asked her along this evening in the hope we could all sit down and try to sort something out.'

Lauren bit down on her bottom lip. 'H-how do you mean?'

Jude decided not to pull any punches. 'Tally's asthma should be fairly well controlled by now, yet somehow it's not. So there has to be a reason, wouldn't you agree?'

Lauren wiped her hands down the sides of her striped pinny, agitation in her jerky movements. 'I know what you're going to say...' She blinked rapidly. 'I have really tried to stop smoking around her. But it can't be just that, can it?' Her gaze swung fearfully between the two doctors.

'Smoking around asthmatics can be lethal.' Jude's expression was grim. 'Has anyone ever taken the trouble to explain to you just what asthma can do to the body, Lauren?'

The young woman bit her lip. 'I don't know. Dr Remington tried once, I think, but I was too worried about Tally to take much in. I know that's no excuse...' She put a shaky hand to her throat. 'Is my smoking killing my little girl? Is that what you're saying, Doctor?'

'Lauren, it's not too late to turn things around.' Kellah's dark eyes glinted a warning at Jude. For heaven's sake! Was he trying to scare this mother out of her wits? 'Obviously, this isn't the best time to talk to you,' she went on gently. 'But we do need to follow through for Tally's sake.'

Lauren's gaze fell and she stared at her hands, her fingers twisting together on the counter top. 'I'll be out of here in a couple of hours...'

Jude's gaze narrowed. 'Would you feel more comfortable if we met at the surgery later, then?'

'Surely we can come up with somewhere a bit more comfortable?' Kellah took matters into her own hands. If Jude didn't like it, tough! 'What about coming to my place, Lauren? It's a townhouse in Ibis Street, number seventeen. I'll leave the outside lights on. We'll have a coffee and chat over the best options for Tally. Is that all right with you?'

Lauren nodded, her shoulders slumping with seeming relief. 'I'll be there.'

'You were a bit hard on her, weren't you?' Kellah's voice held faint censure. They were making their way along the paving slabs outside the roadhouse to his car.

Jude's face hardened. 'Have you ever seen a child die as the result of an asthma attack?'

'No.' Kellah bit the inside of her lip. 'No, I haven't.'

'Then you're lucky.'

Something in his voice made Kellah stop abruptly under the harsh outside lighting and look up at him. She frowned, noticing the sharp lines of strain etched deeply into his face. 'Do you want to talk about it?' she asked quietly.

'No, I don't. If I need to, I'll be sure to let you know.'

Kellah's hands clenched in her pockets. His tone could have frozen boiling water. And she was the one doing him the favour here. She didn't deserve to be the butt of his boorish behaviour.

Wordlessly, they continued across to where he'd left his car. 'Hop in.' Jude gestured vaguely towards the passenger side as he activated the remote. Within seconds, they were settled and buckled into their seat belts. 'Sorry for my churlish response just now.' He paused with his hand on the ignition. 'It was totally uncalled for. I can only say Tally's situation triggered an unfortunate flashback for me and I reacted.'

Kellah swallowed unevenly, suddenly almost painfully aware of the nearness of his body and the tantal-

ising masculine scent that drifted to her on its warmth.
'It's been a stressful day all round,' she managed stiffly.

'No excuse.' He lifted a shoulder as if shrugging off
her gesture of acceptance. 'I'd like to make up for my
lapse. Would you allow me to buy you dinner while we
wait for Lauren?' Looking carefully both ways, Jude
eased the car out onto the highway back to town.

Almost on cue, Kellah's tummy rumbled. She'd eaten
nothing more substantial than a sandwich at lunch. But
eat with Jude Christie? She could only imagine the awk-
wardness of sitting down to a meal with him. She
dragged her thoughts back into line, weighing the situation in her mind.

He'd have to come to her place to meet with Lauren
and if they were to consult over Tally, it would be hell
on wheels if they were hardly speaking. She felt the
words to refuse him outright die on her tongue. 'Actually, I'd planned to get a take-away Italian. You're welcome to come to my place and share it, if you like.'

'That's very generous of you.' He tipped her a lopsided smile. 'I could eat a horse.'

'I'm almost certain they don't serve horse.' Kellah
picked up his light-hearted cue and decided to run with
it. 'I was thinking of veal scallopine and some of their
focaccia.'

Jude made a sound of approval. 'Mind if I make a
special salad to go with it?'

'Feel free. You really do know your way around a
kitchen, then?'

'You sound surprised.'

'Just a bit.' She managed a small laugh. 'My dad
thinks it's totally a female's domain but, then, that's
probably a generational thing. And Will, my brother-in-

law, would be hard pressed to find the teabags, let alone know what to do with them.'

'I find cooking both creative and relaxing.' Jude stopped at the traffic lights. 'I'll cook for you some time—if you'll allow me,' he added gruffly.

'Fine,' she said a bit too heartily. 'But perhaps I should wait until I've tasted your salad.'

Jude's rumble of laughter was rich and warm. 'You're hedging your bets, in other words.' In a spontaneous gesture, his hand slid across and pressed hers where it rested along her thigh. 'I can live with that.'

Kellah took a sharp breath, feeling as though she'd stumbled against an electric wire. Suddenly her whole arm was tingling, her heartbeat in disarray and his car way too small for comfort.

Within a few minutes they were back at the hospital precincts. 'Thanks…' Kellah reached out towards the doorhandle. 'I'll collect our take-away and see you back at my place, then?'

Jude smiled fleetingly. 'My treat next time. I'll cruise the supermarket and get the makings of our salad. Should I bring wine?'

'Ah…no, thanks.' Kellah slid out of the car, turning her head back to him. 'I have a nice merlot on hand.'

For heaven's sake get a grip, Kellah chastised herself silently, all the way home to her apartment, all the way from the carport to the front door and into the kitchen.

You're offering to share a meal with a colleague, nothing more.

Feeling as though her hands belonged to someone else, she slid the scallopine into a serving dish and popped it into the warming oven. 'Wine,' she murmured, flipping the bottle out of the top cupboard. Uncorking it expertly, she left it on the counter top to breathe.

Would she have time to grab a shower and change? She glanced at her watch and her heart began to race. He'd be here in a matter of minutes. Possibly, just. Collecting her jacket and shoulder-bag, she ran up the stairs to her bedroom.

For crying out loud! Jude let his breath go in a slow release of self-admonishment. How could he have let his professional composure slip like that? She'd asked a perfectly natural question. A caring question. And he'd bitten her head off.

He smothered a groan of self-reproach. *You'd better lighten up, Christie, or no one will want to work with you. Kellah Beaumont certainly won't.* But the past had ambushed him out of nowhere. Like a punch to the solar plexus.

Frustration ripped through him as he struggled to find a way forward amongst the chaos of his thoughts.

He'd apologised and she'd accepted. She'd gone further and invited him to share her meal. At the thought his heartbeat quickened. He hadn't imagined the attraction. But maybe he had. He was so out of touch...

He stumbled through the supermarket, hardly knowing what he'd come for. Grabbing stuff at random, he made his way to the checkout.

'It's only a meal, you idiot,' he muttered in self-deprecation, slinging the carry bags into the boot of his car. A meal while they waited to speak to the parent of their young patient. Now he just needed to convince himself of that.

He was familiar enough with the town's layout to find Kellah's apartment block without hassle. Gliding the

Audi to a stop beside the kerb, he cut the engine. For a moment he sat very still, peering through the windscreen at the softly lit street.

The silence was absolute and he was disturbed to find that through it he could hear the thudding of his own heart.

CHAPTER THREE

THE mellow chime of her doorbell had Kellah spinning around, her hand on her heart. Oh, lord, Jude was here already. Her feet felt clad in cement shoes as she went to the door to let him in.

'Hi.' Jude blinked a bit uncertainly. He'd not been prepared for the change in her. Her dark hair was sexily tumbled around her shoulders, her eyes soft and a bit hazy, her jeans and simple white T-shirt clinging so sweetly to her curves.

He felt the tightness in his gut. Hell. He shouldn't have come here…

'Is that our salad?' Kellah indicated the carry bags he was holding out like an Olympic torch.

'Ah…yes,' he said, his voice sounding suddenly rusty and unused. 'I needed some land cress but they didn't have any.' He followed her through to the kitchen.

'Is that the opposite of watercress?' Kellah's face was averted as she reached for a salad bowl out of the top cupboard.

'Mmm…' Jude watched helplessly as her T-shirt rode up from her hipster jeans, revealing the feminine curve of her tummy and a strip of smooth olive skin.

'This do?' She placed the rather battered wooden bowl on the counter.

'That's great.' He shook his head slightly, as if trying to clear his thoughts, catching her look and the slight query in her eyes. 'What?'

She laughed off-key. 'I feel a bit daunted, if you must know.'

Jude tilted his head, his blue eyes narrowing. 'For crying out loud, why?'

She made a vague motion with her hand. 'My kitchen stuff is all a bit dated. It's mostly from Mum's…'

His mouth tilted. 'I much prefer well-loved utensils. And especially I love wooden salad bowls. Do you usually season it with oil after you've used it?'

She nodded, her teeth biting into the softness of her lower lip. 'Anything I can do to help?' she asked quickly, needing something concrete to occupy her mind.

'I think I can manage to toss a few salad greens into a bowl.'

'I'll, um, set the table, then.'

'Don't go to any trouble on my account. I expect you were going to eat off a tray in front of the telly. Am I right?'

She gave a rueful laugh. 'All too often these days, I'm afraid.'

'I can empathise with that.' Jude moved to the sink to wash the lettuce.

Kellah swallowed and her heart began to race. All thumbs, she collected cutlery and place mats from a drawer. 'We'll eat out in the courtyard, then,' she decided breathlessly. 'It's a mild evening.'

'But not for much longer,' Jude predicted, tossing the peppery rocket leaves into the wooden bowl. 'Winter is icumen in.'

Kellah brushed a couple of fallen leaves off the table before setting down her mats and cutlery. If Jilly could see me now, she thought, and suppressed a smile. It was still a touch unbelievable that she had Jude Christie here in her home and was about to share a meal with him.

Suddenly, she realised just how lonely and predictable her evenings had become.

'Right, are you ready for me?' Carrying a tray, Jude stepped out through the French doors into the courtyard. 'I took the liberty of bringing the wine.'

'Lovely.' She felt herself blush like a schoolgirl. 'I'll get the hot food.'

'And some glasses,' he called after her. 'I don't fancy drinking out of our shoes.'

Kellah shot him a laughing look. 'That might be a bit difficult seeing as I'm wearing sandals.'

While Jude poured the wine, she took the lid off the oven dish and released the focaccia with its topping of rosemary and olives from its foil wrapping.

'That smells fantastic.' Jude sniffed appreciatively as they took their places in the comfortable wooden out-door chairs.

'Well, don't stand on ceremony.' Looking at him, at the youthful anticipation in his expression, Kellah tried to still the clamour inside her. She took his glass of wine and handed it across to him. 'This is quite a full-bodied one. I hope you enjoy it.'

'To good food and good friends, then.' He smiled, touching her glass with his. 'And it's my treat next time, remember?'

She was holding herself very still. How could she forget?

'So, how long have you had this place?' Replete, Jude looked at her over the rim of his glass.

'Couple of years.' Kellah wiped her fingers on her serviette. 'I love it but my sister Jillian thinks it's too tiny. She maintains you couldn't swing a cat in the kitchen.'

Jude raised a dark brow. 'Beats me why would anyone want to swing a cat in the kitchen.'

She laughed softly. 'My thoughts exactly.' She paused, cupping her chin in her upturned hand, watching him. 'What about you? Where are you living?'

'About five Ks out of town at Logger's Bend. It's an ancient farmhouse surrounded by a few acres. I acquired it a couple of years ago when I was here visiting Sarah.' His gaze dropped and he grinned a bit sheepishly. 'I bought it for the fabulous old mulberry tree in the back garden.'

'As good a reason as any.'

They exchanged smiles of understanding and then Jude shot jerkily to his feet. 'I'll, uh, help you clear up. Mrs Muir will be here directly.'

Heavens, they were almost being domestic together, Kellah thought with a little pang as Jude rinsed the plates and handed them across to her to stack in the dishwasher. 'I'll wash the glasses separately,' she said, placing them to one side. 'Sure that's everything?'

'Think so.' He took a cursory look around. 'I'll just nip outside and collect the place mats.'

Kellah closed the door on the dishwasher. 'Would you prefer real coffee?' she asked, as Jude tossed the mats on the counter and turned to close the French doors.

'Actually, at this time of night, I prefer a good instant.'

'So do I.'

'Another thing we have in common, then.' He smiled, a grin that changed his expression so much it startled her. She dipped her head, busying herself setting out cups and saucers and reaching down a tin of tiny orange shortbread biscuits. 'We're all set now for when Lauren gets here,' she said to cover the awkward little silence.

Jude spun out a chair from the adjoining dining alcove and sat back to front. He flicked an eyebrow in her direction. 'So, what background do we have on the Muirs? Dad's not around, I take it?'

'No.' Kellah shook her head. 'It's all rather sad. Dane Muir was killed in a mine explosion some years ago. Apparently, the gases were so lethal the management ordered the mine sealed. It was considered no one would have been able to survive.'

Jude blew out a long breath between his teeth. 'That's rough.'

'I think that's the real reason Lauren stays here,' Kellah commented quietly. 'To be near him.'

Jude rubbed his hand across his cheekbones, his eyes staring off into the distance. 'OK, thanks, Kellah,' he said huskily, spinning up from his chair as the doorbell sounded. 'I know what I'm dealing with now.'

Kellah ducked out into the hallway. When she returned with Lauren, Jude had replaced the chair neatly back at the round dining table and was standing behind it, his hands spread across the top.

'Lauren.' He nodded briefly in her direction.

Lauren managed the ghost of a smile and looked uncertainly between the two doctors.

'Make yourself comfortable, Lauren.' Kellah looked at the tired young woman and felt her heart go out to her. 'I'll just get the coffee.'

'I'll get it.' Jude placed a delaying hand on her shoulder. 'You keep Lauren company.'

Lauren sent a guarded look around the room. 'It's very good of you to let me come to your home, Dr Beaumont.'

Kellah waved a hand dismissively. 'For Tally's sake we do need to talk. And what about your own health, Lauren?' she asked gently. 'Are you coping with this added stress?'

'Oh, I just keep going. I mean, you have to, don't you?'

Kellah's mouth drew in slightly. Lauren was far too thin. If she could kick the smoking habit, begin to eat sensibly, put on a little weight...

'Here we are, guys.' Jude placed the tray on the table. 'Coffee for three.' After the slightest pause, he decided to plunge straight in. 'Just for the record, Lauren, you're not on trial here. But obviously we need your input if we're to sort something out for Tally. Do you have any idea what may have triggered her asthma this time?'

'She had a cold.' Lauren kept her gaze averted. 'Sometimes, no matter what I do, she can't seem to throw it off. I know that my smoking doesn't help...' She paused and chewed her bottom lip. 'So I've made a decision to quit.'

'Good for you.' Jude leaned forward earnestly.

'But I'll need help.'

'You'll have it. As a matter of fact, I'm about to start a quit programme at the surgery.'

Kellah flashed him a startled look. This was the first she'd heard of it. Usually, any new initiatives were discussed at their staff meetings before any decisions as to their viability were made. But, then, perhaps Jude had already cleared it with Leo.

'Tally was really sick last night when you came to the house.' Lauren looked across at Jude, her hand clenched across her chest. 'It scared me. And what you said about smoking being lethal...'

Jude gave a smile that was more of a wince. 'I really

did frighten the life out of you, didn't I? Kellah suggested as much.'

Kellah nodded, grateful for his perceptiveness and oddly reassured as well. She said quietly, 'Perhaps it would help if we explained things, Lauren. Give you some idea of what Tally is battling against every time she has one of these episodes.'

'Excellent idea.' Jude flipped a pen out of his shirt pocket. 'Perhaps if I sketched something?' He raised a dark brow in Kellah's direction.

Obligingly, Kellah rose to her feet and fetched a scribble block she kept in the kitchen for her shopping lists.

'Thanks,' Jude acknowledged. Moving a little closer to Lauren, he began sketching an explanatory diagram. 'Typically, asthma affects the lungs. When someone has an attack the tubes begin narrowing, making breathing difficult.'

'That's the wheezing sound Tally makes?' Lauren's fingers tightened around her coffee-cup.

'Yes.' Jude added a few strokes to his diagram. 'And the more she struggles to breathe out, the more the lung collapses and the small amount of space left in the airways is wiped out. Then, as you've probably noticed, she starts to cough.'

Lauren's mouth trembled. 'It's scary.'

'But more so for Tally,' Kellah observed quietly.

Lauren shook her fair head. 'I still don't understand about the breathing thing. I mean, Tally seems to get ill so suddenly.'

'OK.' Jude proceeded to flesh out his drawing. 'This is the lung. All it takes is a trigger for these tiny muscles that surround the air tubes to go into spasm. It can be something as simple as a change in temperature, maybe exercise during her sport at school, animal fur or even certain types of pollen. And, I have to say it, Lauren, *smoke*. All at once Tally begins feeling tight. And I dare say pretty panicky.'

'Oh…' Lauren's eyes overflowed and she swiped at them with the backs of her hands. 'Poor kid. I should've stopped smoking ages ago.'

'I'm sure you'll do it now.' Kellah's tone was carefully neutral. 'And we'll help you all we can.'

Finally, Lauren took a steadying breath and asked, 'Can Tally be cured, if I do everything right in future?'

'Unfortunately not.' Jude shook his head.

'But asthma can be controlled very effectively in the majority of cases,' Kellah was quick to point out.

'To that end, I'll review all her current treatment,' Jude promised. 'Maybe we'll need to make some changes here and there and I'll also put you in touch with the Asthma Foundation. They're very pro-active.'

'They'll let you know about camps and activities Tally can take part in,' Kellah said warmly. 'And she'll meet other youngsters who have varying degrees of asthma so she won't feel the odd one out.'

Jude smiled encouragingly. 'We'll work together on this, Lauren. Pretty soon we'll have both the Muir ladies fighting fit and dangerous.'

Lauren gave a choked laugh. 'I don't know about that.' She blinked rapidly. 'But thank you. I don't know what else to say…'

Saturday morning.

Kellah woke with a feeling of anticipation, something she hadn't experienced for ages. Was it all because of Jude Christie? Just for a moment her heart revved as if an electrical current had been shot through it.

Staring up at the ceiling, she felt a flush heat her

cheeks, her mind drifting back to the previous evening, after they'd seen Lauren safely to her car and then watched her drive off.

The temperature had dropped sharply and Kellah had given a little shiver. 'Come here.' Jude's voice had sounded like a husky echo in her ear, his arm coming around her shoulders, hugging her to his side. 'Let's get you back inside…'

Almost impatiently, Kellah threw back the covers and swung out of bed. She felt light-headed suddenly, as if the oxygen had been sucked out of her lungs.

Her thoughts were spinning as she threw herself under the shower.

Towelling herself dry, she decided she'd dress for comfort. Opening her wardrobe, she pulled out a pair of cargo pants and a candy-striped shirt. As she twisted her hair into a loose knot, she reminded herself to take a shady hat and sunscreen when she went to pick up the children.

'Hi, it's me!' Kellah called the greeting and made her way through the laundry and into the kitchen.

Jilly turned her head from her task at the bench top. 'Oh, good. You're early.' She brushed back an unruly curl with her forearm. 'Thanks for doing this, Kel.'

Kellah smiled wryly. 'And for the umpteenth time, you're welcome. How are my little darlings?'

'Don't ask,' Jilly said darkly, wiping her hands with a paper towel. 'Could you be a love and put the rest of the patty cakes in one of those containers? I have to go and change.'

'Why, for heaven's sake? You look perfectly fine to me.' Kellah eyed her sister's fashionable outfit of white trousers and skinny-rib top and frowned.

Jilly snorted. 'This is why!' She turned from the bench, revealing a red stain down the side of her top and one leg of her trousers.

'Oh, dear.' Kellah bit back a grin. 'What happened?'

Jilly sighed ruefully. 'I was bending over to adjust Gemma's high chair. She lifted her drink at the same moment and the top came off her trainer cup. You can see where the juice landed. And if that wasn't enough, Matty decided to be extra-helpful and grabbed my lace doily off the sideboard—you know the one Mum crocheted for me—and proceeded to mop up everything, including the cat.'

'Oh, lord,' Kellah said gravely, and then chuckled. 'In other words, a good start to your day, was it?'

'And my outfit's ruined!' Jilly wailed. 'The stains will never come out and it cost the earth.'

'Rats,' Kellah reprimanded mildly. 'I've treated much worse stains from the surgery. Go and change. I'll run your stuff through the machine before the kids and I leave for the fête.'

'Oh, Kel, would you?' In a spontaneous gesture Jilly reached out and gave her sister a hug. 'I'll return all these favours when you have kids.'

'Promises, promises.' Kellah looked briefly at the ceiling. 'And speaking of the children, where are they?'

'They're watching a video—a suitable one,' Jilly emphasised, showing Kellah the tip of her tongue before departing to get changed.

She hadn't done this in ages, Kellah thought, finding herself being swept up in the general excitement as she made her way through the gates of the kindergarten.

'I want a go on the merry-go-round,' Matthew stated, sending a melting smile up at his aunty.

'Me, too,' Gemma said around her thumb.

'We've to drop off your mum's cakes and sweets first,' Kellah told them, the large carry bag banging against her leg as she pushed Gemma in her stroller across to where the stalls were set out in a semi-circle.

In a matter of a few minutes, Kellah had fulfilled her official duties. 'Now let's have some fun.' She smiled down at the children. 'Who'd like a balloon?'

'Me, me…'

Almost two hours later, Kellah took a minute to relax, sinking gratefully onto one of the wooden benches scattered around the grounds. She looked down at Gemma in her stroller and smiled. She'd dropped off to sleep. The little pet was worn out.

An elderly woman parked herself beside Kellah, surrounding herself with bags of goodies she'd bought at the stalls. She followed Kellah's gaze to the sleeping Gemma. 'You have a beautiful daughter.' She smiled. 'What's her name?'

'Gemma. And I'm her aunt,' Kellah explained. 'I'm looking after Gem and her brother today. And speaking of her brother…' Kellah was aware of a faint unease. She'd left Matthew enjoying himself on the nearby slippery slide.

She sprang upright. Children moved so quickly. She cast a frantic look around, feeling hot with relief when she saw her nephew amongst a group of children squabbling over the string attached to a shiny helium balloon.

'Oh, lord,' she muttered, and turned to the elderly woman. 'I'd better go and sort this out. Could you keep an eye on Gemma for me?'

The woman nodded and Kellah dived into the swarming group of children. 'Matthew!' She tried to release determined little fingers from the balloon's string.

At the same moment another pair of hands lunged in to grab the other protagonist.

'Zac!' A deep voice cut through the babble.

Straightening up, with Matthew in her arms, Kellah came face to face with Jude.

It was difficult to gauge who was the more surprised.

Kellah was stunned. He held the little boy against his chest, a little boy whose colouring matched Jude's right down to the navy blue eyes... Did he have a child? Her heart thudded. Was the man married? And, if so, what kind of agenda was he running, coming on to her? Even obliquely. 'Yours?' Her throat made a convulsive swallowing movement.

'My nephew, Isaac. His mum's off rehearsing the lead in some darned stupid play.' His smile was fleeting and dry. 'Your nephew, too, I take it?'

Kellah nodded. 'This is Matthew and *his* mum is off directing the darned stupid play.'

Jude's head tipped back in a rough laugh. 'Looks like we're both on kid duty, then. What about time off for good behaviour, Doc? Fancy a cup of tea?'

'Love one,' Kellah said with feeling, then remembered with a pang of guilt that she'd left Gemma with a virtual stranger. 'I just have to grab Matt's sister. She's asleep in the stroller over there.'

'Good grief.' Jude shook his head slightly. 'You're here with two?'

'Oh, they're no trouble,' she offloaded with a laugh.

'Hmm...' Jude stroked his chin, smiling at her across the children's heads. Then his look turned to something else and they continued to stare at each other like two people seeing one another for the first time.

'Ah...' Jude seemed to gather himself. His gaze slid

away and he put Isaac down. 'What about I get an ice cream for these guys while you collect Gemma?'

'That sounds good.' Kellah took a shattered breath. 'They're serving refreshments in the main building. I'll organise my two and meet you there.'

Jude found a table, directing Isaac to one of the chairs and settling him safely. Then he straightened, watching Kellah with her two little charges coming through the louvred timber doors which had been folded back to allow easy access to the refreshment area.

His heartbeat quickened, his gut clenching with a huge uncertainty. Suddenly and without warning, he felt a stab of want, an ache his body hadn't felt for a long time.

Kellah saw Jude on the far side of the room, her heartbeat accelerating wildly, becoming an agitated little flutter against the soft cotton of her shirt. Her thoughts began spinning back and she was reliving the sudden tension between them only moments earlier.

For heaven's sake! she berated herself, but was unable to let go of the sensation. It had been almost suffocating, like being caught in an air pocket of some kind.

Jude sprang to his feet when the little party arrived at the table. 'What about an early lunch?' He felt in his back pocket for his wallet.

'Well…my two have been stoking up on all kinds of treats but I wouldn't say no to a sandwich or something,' Kellah said hesitantly.

'Me neither.' He looked pleased. 'Back in a minute.' He dropped a hand on his nephew's head. 'Stay put, mate.'

'I hope Uncle Jude won't forget the ice creams,' Isaac piped up importantly.

'He won't.' Kellah smiled reassuringly at the handsome little boy. *And how can you be sure of that?* a probing inner voice asked. Kellah settled into the contours of the chair and closed her eyes momentarily.

Somehow, she just knew Jude Christie was a man to rely on.

CHAPTER FOUR

MONDAY.

Kellah blocked a yawn as she lifted her medical case from the passenger seat and alighted from her car. She must be nuts, she thought in disgust, coming to the surgery so early, but there was always something she needed to catch up on. And it was so much easier to do it when the place was quiet.

Besides, she hadn't slept all that well…

Closing the door of the car, she stood for a moment, breathing in the sparkling crispness of a May morning. Yet already the air seemed to hold the foretaste of winter, of frosty mornings, hot soup and cosy night-time fires.

What would this winter bring? Kellah wondered and felt a strange little dip in her stomach when she looked across the car park. 'Oh, lord, he's here,' she murmured under her breath, recognising Jude's distinctive car. So what? She gave a restive little shake of her head, as if to dissipate the faint unease. Obviously, like her, he'd come in early to get caught up on his caseload.

She went in through the rear entrance, unlocking the door of her surgery and shrugging out of her lightweight jacket. She paused. It would be so easy to go along to Jude's office, to pop her head in and casually ask him if he'd like a coffee.

At the very idea, every nerve in her body tightened, became electrified with sensation. She made a little sound of self-derision. She couldn't be casual around

him. She just couldn't. And she'd just better face the
fact and try to stay out of his orbit before she made a
complete fool of herself.

But she needed a coffee to wake up. Well, why not?
The staff kitchen was far enough away from Jude's room
to allow her to get in and out without him being aware
she was even in the building.

Resolutely, she straightened her shoulders and made
her way along the passageway, pushing the door open
and coming to a dead stop.

'Oh. Hi,' she said faintly.

Jude lifted his eyes and acknowledged her presence
with a fleeting parody of a smile.

Kellah blinked. He looked positively grim, as though
he hadn't slept. Without stopping to analyse anything,
she pulled out the chair opposite and sat down. 'What
are you doing here so early?'

He gave a short humourless laugh. 'I could ask the
same of you.'

She palmed a shrug. 'Paperwork.'

'You should learn to delegate.'

'I would if I could. But I like to make sure my notes
are as comprehensive as I can make them. That way, if
I'm run over by a bus I can ensure my patients receive
continuity of care.'

'I must remember that.' He cut their eye contact and
stared down into his coffee-cup.

So he wasn't going to answer her question as to why
he'd come in early. Oh, well. Kellah got to her feet and
went across to the bench. She checked the electric jug
for water and, finding it still almost full, turned on the
power to bring it back to the boil.

Suddenly she changed her mind and decided she'd

have tea. Reaching down a new packet of teabags, she
fiddled with the unfamiliar packaging.

'Here, let me.' Jude scraped back his chair.

Kellah bristled. Damn the man. He'd been watching
her. 'Be my guest.' She tossed the offending packet
aside and bent to open the dishwasher. Taking out a
clean tea-mug, she placed it on the bench top just as
Jude spun up off his chair, his elbow sending her mug
crashing to the floor.

'Why don't you call me a clumsy ox?' he muttered,
as they bent together to pick up the fragments.

'Because you can't swing a cat in this damned space,'
Kellah countered. 'It's like sale day at the cattle yards
when everyone's in here.'

Jude turned his head a fraction, glinting a blue gaze
at her. 'I wondered why you were using the window-
ledge as a coffee-table the other day. In fact, I've wondered about you quite a lot, Kellah…'

'Oh. Her fingers tightened on the shard of crockery in
her hand, the murmured huskiness of his statement sending colour streaming into her cheeks. She looked down,
feeling the thin edge of the shard slice her finger. 'Blast!'
Drawing quickly upright, she edged across to the sink.

'What've you done?' Jude straightened like a spring
uncoiling. 'Show me.'

'I'm OK.' Kellah shouldered him away.

'Let me look, dammit.'

She took a thin breath as her hand was swallowed up
by the strong, blunt fingers that gently examined the tiny
cut. 'You'll live,' he murmured, washing it under the tap
and patting it dry with a couple of tissues from a nearby
dispenser. 'Just let me make sure there's no fragment
embedded.'

Kellah swallowed thickly as he bent over the wound, his head so close, the dark silky strands of his hair almost brushing her temple. With barely centimetres between them, she could have reached out and stroked his face. The fact that she wanted to turned her stomach inside out.

'It shouldn't be a problem—it's stopped bleeding already,' he said.

'I won't need a sick note, then.' Her laugh was jagged, her gaze turning up to meet his, and for a searing moment the atmosphere around them was entirely still.

Jude's look was intense. A husky little sound left his throat and almost in slow motion he released her hand and drew her into his arms.

She took a shattered breath, thought about resisting but clung to him instead, absorbing the unique male feel of him, glorying in the absolute rightness of his arms around her.

'Kellah…?' He lifted her chin, intending only to gauge her reaction. Instead, he found himself stirred beyond belief.

His breath rasped as he cupped her face, his thumbs ever so gently following the contours of her cheekbones. She looked so vulnerable, he thought, frowning down at the tiny flecks like gold dust in her eyes. And her skin— so soft, like velvet.

His chest rose as he breathed in deeply, capturing her fragrance, distinctive, special only to her. Oh, hell. He shook his head. He wasn't nearly ready for this…

For the barest second everything was still, as though the world had stopped breathing, and then his lips were on hers in a series of fleeting, tantalising enquiries.

'So sweet,' he murmured, knowing already that one

kiss would never be enough, that this brief brushing of lips could only fuel the fire that was waiting to be lit.

He dipped his head, tasting the fluttering pulse at her throat before catching her lips again.

Kellah's murmured gasp seemed to spur him on. She could feel the wild throb of his heart against his breast-bone as he gathered her in.

His hands slid down to her waist, urging her closer, and a ragged groan escaped from his throat as their bodies came together, inseparable.

Kellah felt her legs turn to jelly, her heartbeat accel-erating, beating against her chest like the wings of a huge eagle. And her mouth couldn't get enough of him. On a little cry she opened to him and their contact be-came as one life force.

Then suddenly without warning he was pulling back, his breathing harsh and ragged.

'Jude…' She put a hand to her throat, her gaze wide and bewildered.

'Teri's in.' The words were hoarsely spoken, made strident by his shallow breathing. 'She always slams the door off its hinges.'

'Oh!' In a quick protective movement, Kellah pressed the back of her hand to her mouth, feeling the imprint of his kisses return in a wash of quivering nerve-ends. 'What on earth were we thinking of?'

His jaw tightened. 'We were kissing, Kellah. It's hardly a hanging offence.' His hand thrust dismissively through his dark hair. 'Don't take it to heart,' he mut-tered, and turning on his heel he strode out.

Don't take it to heart! When he'd just turned her safe world inside out! Sickeningly conscious of the drumbeat thud of her heart, she watched him go.

'Morning, Jude.'

Kellah hastily rearranged her expression, hearing Teri's chirpy greeting, her light footsteps along the passageway. Bending, she retrieved the last fragments of the broken cup.

'Oh, my gosh!' Teri came through the door and to an abrupt halt. 'You two been throwing the crockery at each other?' Laughing at her own joke, she plonked several packets of biscuits and a carton of milk on the counter top.

'Very funny.' Kellah picked up the broken handle and another piece of china.

'Leave it now, Kel.' Teri shooed her away. 'I'll vacuum the rest of it. There'll be tiny shards you'd never even see. And I'll bring you a cup of tea,' she added, with a grin. 'It's obvious you made a hash of getting your own.'

Kellah fled back to her room as though she were being pursued, still agonising over Jude's parting words. *Don't take it to heart*, he'd said, as if their kisses had meant nothing…

'Thanks.' Kellah looked up, managing a strained smile as Teri arrived with the tea. 'You're in early,' she deflected quickly.

Teri grinned disarmingly. 'I like to get a jump-start on Mondays. I'll have your list ready shortly. Oh, by the way…' the receptionist made a small face and edged against the corner of the desk '…Deidra Meadows rang late on Friday just before I left. Asked for an urgent appointment today. You're fully booked all this week so the best I could do was to slot her in last appointment tomorrow.'

'Was she OK with that?'

Teri shrugged. 'Seemed to be.'

So obviously it wasn't too urgent. Kellah sipped her

tea thoughtfully. Deidra had been her patient for almost a year now.

When she'd first come to the surgery, she'd explained she and her husband Ryan had been trying for a baby for a long time with no success. Kellah had referred the couple to a fertility specialist and after tests Deidra had enthusiastically begun IVF treatment.

Kellah propped her chin on her hand and looked into space. Perhaps there was nothing wrong at all, she decided. Perhaps Deidra had good news at last.

Kellah's mind snapped back to reality at the sound of a commotion outside. Her stomach dived. Just recently they'd had an attempted robbery, an addict demanding drugs—and Teri was on her own out there. She sprang to her feet just as Teri burst through the door.

'Oh, Kellah, can you come?' Teri's eyes were like saucers. 'It's Leo. He's collapsed!'

Kellah sucked in a breath. 'Where is he?'

'In Reception. He asked for his patient list and then his eyes kind of rolled. It was awful…'

'Call an ambulance, Teri,' Kellah directed sharply, her glance sweeping the reception area, relieved beyond words to see Jude was already in attendance.

'Oh, dear heaven,' Kellah breathed, her thoughts flying to Bettina. She and Leo didn't need this on top of everything else. In seconds she was at Leo's side, disposing of his tie and in one sweeping movement popping open the buttons on his pristine white shirt.

Jude was searching for a pulse, his face grim. 'Nothing,' he said shortly.

'I'll get the Oxyviva.' Sophie, who had just arrived, took in the situation and ran.

'And bring the defib!' Jude yelled after her.

Kellah began CPR, her gut clenching at the possible

consequences. Heart attacks were insidious things, striking their victims at random, without warning.

'Keep it going, Kellah.' She heard the urgency in Jude's voice, felt his fingers hard and warm on her shoulder. 'I'll get a line in. Teri?' He arched back, his gaze intense. 'What's the status on the ambulance?'

'On its way.'

'Any pulse?' He swung back to Kellah.

'No.'

He swore under his breath. 'Let's defib, then. What's caused this, do you suppose?' he snapped, placing the pads on the senior partner's chest.

'Stress, probably.'

A muscle worked briefly in Jude's jaw. He switched the life-saving machine on.

Kellah felt the beat of silence almost tangibly while the machine charged.

'Clear!' Jude's deep voice shot through the stillness as he discharged the paddles.

Her lips clamped, Kellah felt for a pulse and shook her head.

'Adrenalin!' Jude barked, and Sophie snapped the prepared dose into his hand.

Please, work, Kellah prayed silently as Jude shot the stimulant home and prepared to defib once more.

'All clear. Shocking!'

'We have a pulse,' Kellah confirmed. 'And spontaneous breathing.'

Jude's expression cleared. 'About bloody time.'

'Here's the ambulance.' Sophie ran to the entrance to let the officers in through the heavy plate-glass doors.

'I'll get hold of Bettina.' Kellah stood aside as the ambulance stretcher was snapped into place.

Jude's dark head swung up in query. 'Can she cope just now?'

'She'll cope,' Kellah asserted. 'She's a strong lady. She has a sister living nearby as well. I'm sure she'll support Bettina any way she can.'

'I'll go with Leo, then.' Jude kept his hand on their senior colleague's shoulder as the trolley was wheeled out. 'I'll let you know the minute I have some news.'

'Take care.'

'You, too.' Jude's look was brief and intense, before he turned and followed the ambulance officers out through the doors.

Within a few minutes Tony and Maggie had arrived at the surgery and the shocked staff members drew close together in consultation.

'Have you managed to get hold of Bettina?' Tony threw the sombre question at Kellah.

She shook her head. 'This is something I need to tell her in person, I think. I'll go now.' She glanced at her watch. 'How long before my first appointment, Teri?'

'You've time. I can stall anyhow. What should I do about Leo's patients?'

'Normally, Jude would see them.' Tony rubbed a hand around his jaw. 'You'd better phone them all, Teri. Explain there are only two doctors on duty. If they're prepared to wait, we'll see them when we can, but otherwise give the option of rescheduling.'

'I'll help,' Maggie said practically. 'We'll juggle the lists around somehow.'

Kellah raised a dark brow at Tony. 'Perhaps we'd better schedule an emergency staff meeting for lunchtime. Jude should be back by then.'

Tony nodded. 'Obviously, we'll have to throw him in

at the deep end now, but I have no doubt he'll cope. Thank heaven you were both in early, otherwise—'

'Don't go there.' Kellah suppressed a shudder. 'We just have to pray now that Leo will pull through.'

Kellah ran a brush through her hair and added a dash of lipstick. The morning surgery hadn't run much overtime and their patients had co-operated marvellously.

Jude had rung from the hospital as he'd promised. Leo had suffered a relatively mild MI. He was listed as serious but stable. 'Bettina's arrived so I don't think I need hang about,' Jude had said. 'But I'll look in on Tally while I'm here. That should save a bit of time later. I guess you've patients coming out of the woodwork?'

'Isn't it always the way?' Relief at Leo's prognosis put a lightness in Kellah's response. 'It'll be good to have you back, Doctor.'

His chuckle was rueful. 'Thanks—I think.'

Kellah was smiling as she put the phone down. Thank heaven he'd lightened up. But then her look became shuttered. She thought of how he had held her. Kissed her. How could he have shut down on his emotions so quickly afterwards? She swung up off her chair. Why were relationships never straightforward?

With her usual efficiency, Maggie had arranged for sandwiches to be brought in from the local deli and had topped up the coffee-maker in readiness.

'The jug's just boiled if anyone would prefer tea,' she said.

'I would, thanks, Maggie.' Jude strode in, dumping several files on the table.

'Good work this morning, you two,' Tony said around a mouthful of cheese and pickle sandwich. 'I thought

Leo looked a bit grotty a week or so ago. I offered to give him a check-up. He hit the roof.'

Kellah lifted a shoulder. 'Do you know any medicos who take their own health seriously?'

'I read recently one Australian dies every ten minutes from cardiovascular disease,' Maggie said soberly. 'Poor Leo.' She shook her head. 'I hope he'll recover fully. I was with him when he first opened this practice, you know—he and Bettina. She was his nurse for ages…'

'I spoke to the attending cardiologist a short while ago, Maggie,' Jude said kindly. 'Things are looking positive.'

'Oh, good.' Maggie picked up her mug of herbal tea. 'I'll leave you to get on with your meeting, then. I'm sure you've lots to sort out.'

'So, Jude.' Tony hunched forward, his hands spanning his coffee mug. 'How is he really?'

'They're giving Leo anti-hypertensive drugs IV and he's on constant ECG to monitor any changes.'

Tony nodded. 'What's the short-term prognosis?'

'As you'd expect. Wait and see. Dr Chalmers said they'll carry out the usual exercise and stress tests in a couple of days.'

'He's never smoked, so that's in his favour,' Kellah said hopefully. 'But, of course, recently he's worked himself up into quite a state over Bettina's illness.'

Tony looked grim. 'Well, one thing's certain. He won't be back at work for a while. Which means you're on staff permanently, Jude—if you want to be, of course.'

'Yes, I would—if it's fine with both of you.'

'I couldn't be more pleased,' Tony said sincerely.

'Kellah?' Jude's mouth flattened into a brief smile. 'Do I have your approval as well?'

She spun her gaze up to look at him, losing herself in the luminosity of his blue eyes. She swallowed unevenly. 'Yes, of course.'

For much of the day, Leo's sudden illness placed a dampener on the whole staff. But then, as if by silent mutual consent, everyone worked harder at keeping the atmosphere around the surgery as close to normal as possible.

When she was finished for the day, Kellah took her case from its locker and made her way along the passageway to the staffroom. As she'd half expected, Jude and Tony were already there.

'Need me for anything?' She tossed a questioning look between the two males.

Tony shook his head. Jude, she noticed, looked broodingly away. Her mouth tightened. She'd give a week's salary to find out what was going on in his head. 'I'm just popping over to the hospital, then.'

'Give Leo my best,' Tony said. 'I'll look in on him first thing tomorrow morning.'

'I'll tell him.' Kellah's chin went up sharply. 'I'll see you both in the morning.'

'Hang on a tick, Kellah.' Jude got to his feet and pushed his chair in. 'Tony and I feel it would be a good idea to have a quick meeting each afternoon for the next little while, just to make sure things are on track. Are you OK with that?'

Kellah felt her cheeks warm. 'Well, it would have been nice to have been included in your deliberations but, yes, barring emergencies, I should be able to make it.'

'There was no disrespect intended, Kellah,' Tony was

quick to point out. 'Jude and I just got to talking, that's all.'

'Fine.' Kellah lifted a shoulder. 'See you.' She turned away. Suddenly she needed air.

Kellah got out of the shower and towelled her hair dry. What a very mixed day it had been and it was so good to be home. Pulling on drawstring pants and a T-shirt, she began to blow-dry her hair.

I feel almost human again, she thought with relief, going through to the kitchen. As she poured herself a glass of wine, she knew she could look forward to a quiet night. These days patients needing to see a doctor outside surgery hours were encouraged to go to the newly formed after-hours GP clinic attached to the hospital.

Although all GPs were expected to take a rota of duty there, even make house calls if necessary, it certainly lessened the time they needed to be on call. Which suited her, Kellah decided, lifting her glass and taking a mouthful of ice-cold Riesling. Now she was ready to curl up on her favourite chair and just enjoy the silence for a while.

When her phone rang, she groaned in resignation. It was Jilly on the other end of the line.

'So, who's the dark horse?' she said without preamble.

'Sorry?' Kellah was taken aback.

'Jude.' Jilly was blunt. 'Matthew's been talking about him since the kindy fête on Saturday. Said he bought ice creams.'

Kellah clicked her tongue. 'For heaven's sake! Jude Christie is a new doctor at the surgery. He was looking after his nephew and I had your two. We ran into each other at the fête.'

'And?'

'And nothing,' Kellah said flatly. 'We had a cup of tea and by then the kids were tired and grizzly so we left and went our separate ways.'

'Oh.' Jilly sounded disappointed. 'And there was I thinking you had a new man.'

'There are other things on my mind besides looking for men,' Kellah said, and went on tell Jilly about Leo's heart attack.

'Oh, that's dreadful. Bettina and Leo seem such a nice couple. They always come to our plays,' she added inconsequentially. 'What will happen now? Leo was taking extended leave, wasn't he?'

'Mmm. If the damage to his heart isn't too great, he'll no doubt go on a rehab programme and if he listens to his doctors, he should be back to feeling fit again quite soon. But I imagine they'll still go on their holiday.'

Stripped to the waist, Jude lifted the axe and split another log of firewood. Hell, he was all kinds of a fool. Why on earth hadn't he kept his hands to himself? He'd all but jumped on Kellah. But kissing her had felt so good. So bloody wonderful.

The memory of her feminine softness under his hands made his body tighten even now. Damn. It had been so frustratingly long. No wonder his responses were on a hair-trigger.

He wiped the sweat off his forehead with his forearm and slung the axe aside. If he kept on at this rate, he'd have cut enough wood to last several winters. Turning away from the pile, he took the back steps two at a time and went through the screen door, slamming it shut.

He looked around the kitchen as if disorientated, then shook his head. Going across to the fridge, he took out a can of lager, pulling off the ring-top and downing the first couple of mouthfuls with satisfaction.

His shoulders lifted in a huge controlling breath. Recognising his need to unwind, he wandered out to the front verandah to watch the last of the sunset.

But he couldn't stop thinking about Kellah. He closed his eyes and groaned softly. He was drawn to Kellah Beaumont like a magnet to iron. Would it be so wrong to pursue it? But on the other hand, could he trust himself not to make a hash of things? The last thing he wanted was to hurt her.

But surely the grief was fading.

Eyes half-closed, he watched the trail of pink clouds as the sun cast its setting rays over the canopy of pale blue sky.

Perhaps things would be clearer tomorrow.

Perhaps...

CHAPTER FIVE

BY THE time Kellah had dealt with a very busy surgery list, she'd almost forgotten Deidra Meadows was her last appointment for the day.

Going to the water-cooler in her room, she helped herself to a long cold drink. Perhaps it was nothing more than Deidra popping in to say she's pregnant, she mused hopefully.

But when her patient walked through the door, Kellah instinctively knew it was going to be a difficult consultation. Deidra was tense and serious.

'Come in, Deidra, and take a seat.' Kellah gave her what she hoped was a reassuring smile. 'What can I do for you?'

'Thank you for seeing me.' Deidra Meadows brought her chin up almost defiantly and met Kellah's gaze without expression. 'I just wanted you to know I've opted out of the IVF programme.'

'I see.' Kellah's response was carefully controlled. 'Are you just having a break or—'

'No. It's finished. Over. I won't go through that again.'

Kellah frowned slightly. Surely Deidra wasn't blaming her for the referral? 'I'm sorry it didn't work out for you, Deidra. Really sorry. But you know we talked about this—that IVF doesn't work for everyone.'

The young woman huffed a bitter laugh. 'I've had the most miserable year of my life. Fooling around with my hormones almost turned me into a raving lunatic. It's

like PMT all the time…' She swallowed. 'You feel like
you're living in a knife drawer. And I've put Ryan
through the wringer, demanding sex because it was the
right time. And then…' She bit hard on her bottom lip.
'Then comes a negative pregnancy test and you're both
devastated all over again.'

Kellah's professional instincts sharpened. 'So, what
are your plans now?'

'Please, don't mention adoption.' Deidra held her
hands up in a blocking gesture. 'It's not for me. I don't
want someone else's child.'

Kellah reached out and let her fingers rest briefly on
Deidra's wrist. 'I know it probably sounds like a plati-
tude, but I'm sincerely sorry you've been left with such
negative feelings about IVF.'

'It's not your fault, Dr Beaumont…' Tears clumped
on the young woman's lashes and she swiped them
away. 'I'm determined to get my life back on track, re-
gain my sense of humour at least. And to that end I'm
having a complete change of scene. I'm going to work
in Japan.'

Kellah was taken aback. 'When are you leaving?'

'Next week. My firm is setting up a new branch in
Tokyo. I'm to be the PR person. I've being learning the
language for the past several years so I'm the logical
choice.' She gave a bitter-sweet smile. 'And perhaps
there is an up-side to all this. If I'd got pregnant, this
job would never have been offered to me, would it?'

And you probably wouldn't have wanted it anyway,
Kellah thought heavily. She drummed up a passable
smile. 'Well, congratulations! I hope it works out won-
derfully for you and Ryan.'

'Oh, Ryan's not coming.' Deidra's little shrug was

almost defensive. 'We're separating—at least for now. I don't want him tied to me if I can't give him a child.'

'And what does Ryan think about your decision?' Kellah felt compelled to ask.

Deidra's smile was brittle. 'My contract is for a year. Maybe we'll reassess things then. But in the meantime I'm giving him an out.'

Whew!

Kellah felt slightly shell-shocked when her patient had left. She didn't think she'd ever forget the haunted look on Deidra's face when she'd said she and her husband were separating.

And it was obvious she'd just lost a patient off her list. Deidra had made it plain enough she was through with doctors.

Sighing, Kellah looked at her watch. Oh, lord! She'd probably kept Jude and Tony waiting for ages. In an end-of-day gesture, she raised her arms, dragging her fingers through her hair and shaking it out as she hurried along the passage way towards the staffroom.

'Sorry I'm late.' Pushing open the door, she stopped short. Jude was the only one present.

He spun round from looking out the window. 'Tony sent his apologies. One of his midwifery patients has gone into pretty swift labour. He's at the hospital.'

'So there's just you and me.'

A guarded smile edged itself across his mouth. 'Looks like it. You OK?' he added as an afterthought.

'So-so.' Kellah rocked her hand. 'Tea, coffee or a cold drink? There's bound to be juice or something here.' She went across to the fridge.

'Why don't we get shot of the place and go some-where a bit more conducive to relaxing?'

A beat of silence.

'You've read my mind. And I know just the place.' Kellah heard her voice, oddly calm, and wondered fleetingly how it was possible when just being around Jude turned her equilibrium on its head.

Outside in the car park, Jude stopped beside his Audi and swung his case into the boot. 'I imagine you'll want to take your own car, so I'll follow.'

'This is one of your regular haunts,' Jude surmised when the pleasant middle-aged owner of the little restaurant-cum-coffee-shop greeted Kellah by name and showed them to a snugly private booth.

'Carol's the mum of one of my school friends,' she admitted, shifting her position slightly so she could face him.

A fleeting frown touched his forehead. 'Chadwick is your home town, I take it?'

She nodded. 'My parents had a property a few Ks out. That's where Jilly and I grew up. But neither of us wanted a life on the farm. Jilly went off and acquired a degree in fine arts and married Will Anderson.'

'And you went off and acquired a medical degree and didn't marry anyone.'

Kellah gave a slight lift to her shoulders and a determined smile. 'Yet.'

'Anyone in mind?'

'Perhaps.'

Idiot. Jude squirmed inwardly. Why on earth had he asked her that? 'Uh, do your parents still live locally?' he sidetracked abruptly.

'No. They've retired and moved to the Sunshine Coast. Coolum, to be exact.'

'So, what are we having?' he asked a little too heartily, picking up the menu and making a pretence of studying it.

Kellah's mouth turned down. 'Frankly, I feel the need of some comfort food. My last patient rather socked it to me.'

'I thought you seemed a bit rattled.' Jude's gaze travelled over her face and dropped to the curve of her breast.

'Hi, I'm Rachel.' A smiling young waitress appeared beside their table. 'Are you ready to order?'

'Ah…we'll have cappuccinos, please,' Jude referred to the menu. 'And raisin toast with lashings of butter.'

Kellah rolled her eyes. 'Are we on a cholesterol kick here?'

'You said comfort food.'

'So I did.'

They shared a tentative smile, then suddenly something changed, as if the world tilted just marginally on its axis, and their smiles slipped, turning into something else entirely.

'So…what was the problem with your patient?' Jude drew in a deep breath, a wave of urgency rocking him to the core, causing him to seek a more comfortable position in his chair.

In the subdued lighting Kellah regarded him for a moment—the rather hawk-like features, the tanned column of his throat, his shoulders broad under the soft cotton shirt. She moistened her lips. 'It was a young woman who'd been trying to become pregnant on the IVF programme.'

'Didn't work, I take it?' Jude looked up and thanked the waitress as she placed their cappuccinos on the table.

'She's very bitter.' Kellah took up the teaspoon from

her saucer, absently scooping it through the froth on her coffee.

'Well, it's hardly your fault it didn't take.'

'I felt terrible—as though I shouldn't have referred her and her husband in the first place. And now they're separating.'

Jude's dark brows lifted. 'Pretty shallow relationship, then, if the failure of the IVF was all it took.'

Kellah looked pensive. 'I'd bet my boots it's not what they really want at all. I feel like I've failed them…'

He frowned. 'Kellah, I feel sorry for the couple, but you can't go second-guessing everything you do in medicine. What about adoption? Did you canvass that?'

'I didn't get a chance to. My patient shot that possibility down in flames before I could even bring it up.'

'What the hell is wrong with these people?' Jude's expression closed in anger. 'There are children all over the world just existing, stuck in orphanages, waiting for someone generous enough to open their hearts and love them. To give them a home, a family. A future. God!' He raked his fingers roughly through his hair. 'Don't start me.'

The emotional charge his short outburst had created was mercifully diffused by the arrival of their raisin toast.

Kellah didn't know where to look but she felt compelled to say something. 'Overseas adoption is not for everyone, Jude. It takes rather special people.'

'Would you consider it?' The words were curt, forced out.

'I can't answer that,' she said frankly. 'I've never been in the position where I had to consider it. Would you?' She threw the proposition right back at him.

He looked suddenly bleak. 'We wanted to. Expected to. For lots of reasons it didn't happen.'

We? What was he saying? Kellah felt as though she'd been hit between the eyes. It was a tiny word with only two letters yet it conjured up a thousand questions. Cautiously, unsure how he would react, she said quietly, 'Look—nothing heavy—but do you want to talk about it?'

'No.' He squeezed his eyes shut for a second. 'Maybe some time.'

Without thinking, she reached out her hand and touched his arm. 'I'm sorry.'

His muscles clenched and it was as though a shutter closed suddenly behind his eyes. 'Don't be. It's ancient history.'

But, of course, it wasn't. How could it be, when it was still affecting him so keenly?

And she didn't have to be clairvoyant to see Jude was carrying some kind of very private pain. Fighting some highly disturbing memories.

Thoughtfully, she picked up a piece of toast and nibbled on it. Well, if he didn't want to talk about the past, perhaps he'd be more forthcoming about the present. She was darned if she'd let him crawl back into his dark hole of retrospection.

'So, is Sarah your only sibling?'

Jude's wry look indicated he'd seen right through her little ploy. He lifted his coffee and took a mouthful. 'I have a younger brother. He's married, and they have two delightful little daughters. He works out of Washington for the ABC.'

Kellah's brows rose. 'He's a journalist, too?'

'Mmm. We ended up with two journalists and one doctor in the family. My parents live in Toowoomba.

Dad's a surveyor with the City Council and Mum is a devoted wife, mother and grandmother.'

'What a fabulous influence she must be.'

Jude's look softened. 'She is. This place has a very pleasant atmosphere,' he added casually. 'I must remember to come here again.'

Kellah looked around at the low-key style of the décor, the patina of old wooden furniture, the glow from the copper lanterns. 'Carol's recently had a revamp. Most of the artwork is Jilly's inspiration, actually.'

'Clever.' Jude considered the vivid splashes of green paint on red canvas.

Faintly amused, Kellah followed his gaze. 'She says she prefers to paint emotions rather than images.'

'I can see the idea would have possibilities.' Jude's mouth kicked up in a twisted smile. 'Imagine what we could throw together after a bad day at the surgery.'

Well, at least she'd got him to lighten up, Kellah thought, and tried to ignore the little flutter of hope in her heart. She looked out through the big plate-glass window to the street. The afternoon had drawn in and already the streetlights were dotting their pools of light over the pavement.

She swallowed the last of her coffee and supposed they should make a move but she was loath to break the tenuous kind of peace they seemed to have found.

'What the hell was that?'

Jude's soft expulsion of alarm had Kellah snapping back to the present and jerking a look behind her towards the kitchen.

As she did so, she heard the noise that Jude had noticed first. A muted kind of scream followed by a commotion that could only indicate something was wrong.

'Come on!' Jude whirled to his feet, yanking chairs out of the way as he made a beeline towards the kitchen.

Kellah followed, a knot of unease already forming in her stomach.

'What's happened here?' Jude's voice rang with authority as he strode through into the kitchen.

'Gary's cut his hand.' Rachel spun round, her eyes wide with panic. 'Carol's gone out.'

'OK, let's all just keep calm.' Jude moved swiftly towards the young man in a chef's uniform who was clutching a hand to his chest. Blood was flowing freely down over his forearm.

Kellah winced. 'I'll get my bag.' She turned and ran.

'Take it easy, mate.' Jude eased the young man onto a high stool.

'It hurts like hell…' Gary's forehead was beading with sweat.

'I know.' Jude was gentle. 'I'm a doctor. Let me see the damage. Rachel, could you grab a clean towel, please?'

'Should I call an ambulance?' Rachel was all but wringing her hands.

'Just hang on a minute.' Jude examined the wound, seeing at once that it was deep and jagged but at first glance it appeared no tendons were involved. 'How did you do it, Gary?'

'Deboning a turkey.' He breathed in hard through his clenched teeth. 'Knife slipped. I feel crook, Doc…'

'Right, Gary, I'm just going to pop this oxygen mask on you.' Kellah had returned with her medical case and taken a swift inventory of the situation. 'Breathe away. Good. Feeling more comfortable now?'

The young chef nodded vigorously.

Jude had staunched the bleeding. 'It's not too bad,

actually.' He released the pressure on the wound to allow Kellah to gauge its severity.

She looked at the cut and then raised her head in query. 'Should we get him to Casualty?'

Jude's mouth folded in. 'Apparently they're down on staff today. Gary could possibly have a long wait.'

And by the look of him, he wasn't up to it. Kellah lifted a shoulder. 'Back to the surgery, then. I'll suture, if you'll assist?'

'Such a lack of respect for your elders.' Jude shook his head but gave a twisted smile. 'OK, then, Gary. We'll take you back to our surgery and stitch you up. Can you manage to walk out to my car?'

Kellah snapped the locks shut on her case. 'Rachel, will you be OK here until Carol gets back?'

The young waitress nodded. 'It's a bit early for the dinner crowd and, thank goodness, no other customers have arrived in the meantime.' She swallowed convulsively. 'Will Gary be all right? He looked so pale...'

'He'll be fine.' Kellah wound a reassuring hug around Rachel's shoulders. 'How about you, though? Are you feeling up to coping?'

The youngster took a deeply determined breath. 'I'll be fine. I don't want to lose this job. Carol's so great to work for.'

'Gary's going to be off work for a while,' Kellah said gently. 'What will you do about a replacement chef?'

'At a pinch Carol will probably manage the cooking herself.' Rachel looked around uncertainly. 'But then we'll need someone to help wait on the tables...'

Kellah began to move towards the door. She hated to leave the young woman on her own but right now her medical skills were needed elsewhere. 'I'll phone when we've finished with Gary and let you know how he is,' she promised.

Almost an hour later, Kellah tied the last suture and straightened to survey her work.

'That was very neat.' Jude was generous in his praise. In fact, it was brilliant. With supple skill she'd meticulously brought the edges of the cut together. Almost with a surgeon's precision, he decided as he sealed the whole site with plastic skin to prevent infection.

Kellah stripped off her gloves and tossed them into a disposal bin. 'We'll need you to come back in a week for a check-up, Gary. Quite likely the stitches will be able to come out then.'

Expertly, Jude tied a sling, elevating the young man's hand against his chest. 'That should keep you more comfortable. I'd say you're looking at being off work for a week or so.'

'Doesn't matter.' Gary lifted a shoulder. 'I gave in my notice tonight.'

'You're leaving the restaurant?' Kellah turned sharply from washing her hands at the basin.

'I need more variety,' the young man explained. 'Carol's a good boss and all but I need the experience of working in a larger place. I've been offered a job at the Leagues club. Start in two weeks.'

Jude raised an eyebrow. 'When did you last have a tetanus jab, Gary?'

'I'm up to date. Have to be in my job.'

'I imagine you do. Well, that looks like you sorted, then. Except for some painkillers. We'll give you something just to get you over the next few days. But use the tablets according to directions only,' Jude emphasised.

'If you're worried about anything connected with your wound, contact the surgery—OK?'

'Yeah. Thanks, Doc.' Gary took a couple of steps, swaying slightly. 'I…don't feel all that brilliant. Reckon you could call me a cab to get home?'

'Are we ever going to get shot of this place?' Jude growled, as they turned to go back inside, the cab containing their patient having just pulled away. 'I seem to be spending most of my waking hours here.'

'Don't you dare give *your* notice in, Jude Christie.' Kellah pushed open the door of the surgery and came to an abrupt halt.

'Miss me, would you?'

She looked up, feeling the intensity of that blue gaze. 'Of course the practice would miss you,' she said, deliberately running interference across his question.

He smiled but it was nothing deeper than an enigmatic curve of his lips. 'You're a hard woman, Dr Beaumont.'

Of course she wasn't. Kellah suddenly felt hopelessly out of her depth. Agitatedly, she ran her hands up and down her upper arms. 'I'll, um, just tidy up the treatment room…'

'Leave it for Sophie to do in the morning,' he said, frowning slightly. 'For crying out loud, Kellah, delegate.'

She licked her lips. 'Yes—all right.'

Jude had bent towards her to emphasise his point, his gaze for once gentle.

Kellah swallowed uncomfortably, in that instant sensation flooding her. Yet at the same time something cleared in her mind. A feeling she'd experienced almost since the moment she'd met Jude.

As though she ached for him to pull her hungrily into his arms and never let her go.

'What is it?' His query was throatily soft.

Her heartbeat revved. He'd stepped closer, his mouth just a breath away from hers. For a brief intense moment their gazes locked—and fused.

It was too much for Jude. Not stopping to analyse his thoughts, he reached out and gathered her in. *I should run a mile*, he berated himself silently, before his lips came softly down and closed over her tiny sigh.

In a second they were on fire for one another.

Every nerve-end responsive, Kellah took her time, savouring the feel of his mouth over and over, storing the memory.

She made a little sound in her throat and her fingers found their way to the back of his neck, rode the corded muscle, feathered through his dark hair.

A convulsive shudder ran through Jude as his hand roved across the bare skin at her waist under her shirt, his fingers moving higher, to play down the ridges of her backbone. Yet all at once he knew for his own sanity he had to break the exquisite contact. He drew back from her abruptly, his breathing shallow.

Kellah felt bereft. Like a rag doll, her hands fell to her sides. He'd done it again. Switched off, as if he could only allow himself to go so far and no further. She felt her heart squeeze tight. If he was trying to confuse her, he'd succeeded. She fought for self-preservation, swallowing the dryness in her throat. 'Um…I should go. I want to pop in on Carol.'

Jude caught her hand as she made to step away from him and halted her flight. 'Kellah, don't.'

She bit her lips, her gaze uncertain. 'Don't what?'

'Pretend nothing's happened between us.'

She gave a quiet snort. 'Exactly what has happened between us, Jude? A few kisses that you appear to regret two seconds later?' She licked her lips, tasting him all over again. 'It's…getting late. I have to go.'

Turning on her heel, she shot out the door before Jude could do or say anything more that would place her even further under his spell.

That night Jude's arms felt empty. He lay on his back, staring at the dappled moonlight on the ceiling. And thought of Kellah.

He gave a snort of self-derision. Just the thought of her was enough to make him burn and ache for her. Yet he'd let her walk away confused and hurt.

But the saner part of him was winning, telling him he should butt out now before he dragged her into something that would have the capacity to hurt her even more.

On a muffled curse, he turned the pillow over, thumping it into shape. It didn't help.

He groaned softly with frustration.

Sweet God, she was amazing. She kissed like a dream. Sexy and sweet all bound up together. Even now he could still taste her. And solely because of her, his life had altered in ways he could not have imagined as recently as a month ago.

For the longest time loneliness had become his shadow. He swallowed the sudden constriction in his throat. Dare he take a chance and let the sun in?

CHAPTER SIX

IT WAS the following afternoon.

Heart thumping, Kellah knocked on the door of Jude's consulting room and popped her head in. 'It's only me.' She had difficulty in getting the words past her throat. 'Teri said you were between patients.'

'Kellah…' Jude swung to his feet. 'I was intending to look in on you before surgery this morning.'

'Oh.' After the way they'd parted last night, she doubted that. So, what was his agenda now? The hollow feeling in her stomach intensified.

'Have a seat.' He waved her to a chair and resumed his own.

'Thanks. Um, I wanted to put you in the picture about something I've done.' She rushed into speech.

Jude's head snapped up. 'You haven't gone and chucked your job in, have you?'

Over a few kisses? She shook her head at the absurdity of the thought. Arrogant man. 'Please. You're way off base.'

'I'm glad of that.' Jude couldn't believe the relief he felt. 'So…' He gave her a tight smile. 'What have you done?'

'I've put Carol in touch with Lauren Muir. They were meeting this morning.'

'Sorry…' Jude shook his head. 'Am I being thick?'

Kellah made a click of exasperation. 'Carol's going to offer Lauren a job as her chef. Well, Gary won't be back,' she justified with a little shrug.

Jude looked at her and then blinked. 'That's very pro-active, I must say. You're quite a mover and shaker when you set your mind to it, aren't you?'

Her mouth folded in primly. 'It makes sense. A job with Carol will give Lauren a gentler working environment for starters. She'll have less distance to travel to her job, and the hours and conditions will better suit her situation by a long chalk.'

Jude spread his hands. 'We just have to hope the two will get on.'

'Carol and Lauren?' Kellah gave him an old-fashioned look. 'Carol's one of the warmest people I know. I'm sure she'll take Lauren right under her wing. It'll work out,' she insisted, when Jude still looked sceptical.

'Well, good then.'

A beat of silence.

'Kellah…'

'Jude…'

They both stopped and waited for the other to speak again. 'You first,' she got in quickly.

'I'd like to try to clear the air between us.' His head lifted, dark brows meeting in the centre of his forehead. 'Maybe I shouldn't have kissed you but—'

'Don't worry about it,' she said, cutting him off. 'It doesn't matter.'

The corner of his mouth twitched. 'Of course it matters.'

'I kissed you back,' she reminded him softly.

'So, are you saying we should put it down to chemistry?'

'Or proximity,' she said, which was a much safer thought. And perhaps they could put it down to that, if only she could forget the feel of his mouth on hers, the sensation of his body against her own, the touch of his hands on her bare skin...

And the fact that she wanted more—far more. Much more than he was obviously prepared to give.

'Uh...I have a patient due.' Jerkily she got to her feet and pushed her chair back.

'Lauren's booked to see me this afternoon.' Jude lifted a dark brow. 'Like to sit in?'

She shook her head. 'Patients wall to wall. Fill me in later.'

Jude watched her go, the ache inside him as big as a truck. He wanted her and, without being indecently smug, he knew she wanted him.

Swivelling on his leather chair, he rose to his feet, stretching his six-foot frame to ease the tension in his muscles and walking across to the window.

Perhaps he could begin a kind of courtship of her, he thought, dragging his hands through his hair and locking them at the back of his neck. He snorted over the old-fashioned concept.

Romance her, then?

He smothered a hollow laugh. Did he even know the basics any more?

When his phone rang, he let out a controlled sigh and returned to his desk. He flipped up the receiver. 'Christie.'

'Hi, big brother.'

'Sarah.'

'I need your copy.'

'Ah.' Jude dropped back into his chair, squeezing his eyes shut and pinching his thumb and forefinger across the bridge of his nose. 'When do you need it?'

'Tonight, latest. Can you email it to me at home?'

'Actually, it's not quite finished.'

'Jude…!' Sarah's obvious frustration ruffled across the line. 'What's the problem?'

He couldn't tell her the whole thing was boring him to tears. 'I'm not sure I'm the person for this column thing. Most of the questions read like lifestyle stuff.'

'Well, that's not too difficult, is it?'

'I don't feel like trailing through other people's emotional garbage, Sarah.'

'For heaven's sake!' Sarah clicked her tongue. 'Just keep it light. It's easy enough to do.'

He gave a rough laugh. 'You do it, then.'

'Looks like I'll have to, doesn't it?' she said ruefully. 'Seeing you've turned wimp on me.'

'I'm not opting out completely,' he defended. 'Any time you need me for medical input, I'm available, OK? Just leave me out of the ''what kind of bed should I buy now my girlfriend's moving in'' stuff.'

Sarah cackled. 'Did someone actually ask that?'

'You'd better believe it.' There was a creak of leather as Jude leaned forward abruptly in his chair. He'd noticed the light blinking on his phone dial, indicating his next patient had arrived. 'Sarah, I have to go. I'll send you what I've got.'

'Thanks. Oh—before you rush off. I'll let you have a couple of tickets to my play.'

'Sarah, no offence, but I don't *do* plays. Anyhow, I don't have anyone to invite.'

'Don't be pathetic. What about that cute receptionist at your surgery?'

He snorted inelegantly. 'She's hardly out of school uniform.'

'And you'd merely be inviting her to see a play,' Sarah countered pithily. 'Come along to the final per-

formance and you can join us afterwards for the cast
party. It'll be fun.'

He'd rather stick needles in his eyes, Jude thought
grimly. But, of course, he couldn't hurt his sister by
telling her that. 'I'll think about it, all right? Now I have
to go. Take care.'

Returning the receiver to its cradle, he swung to his
feet and went to greet his next patient.

'Lauren. Come on in.' Jude held the chair for her.
'How are things?'

'Not bad, actually.' Lauren looked as though she
could hardly contain her excitement. 'I have a new job.'

'Ah!' Jude flashed her a knowing smile. 'Dr
Beaumont mentioned something about that. Your inter-
view went well, then?'

The young woman nodded. 'I can't tell you how much
I'm looking forward to getting away from the roadhouse.
Some days I swear I feel I'm on a conveyor-belt of steak
and chips. Now I'll be able to experiment a bit. Carol
has quite a varied menu.'

'Well, I'm glad it's all turned out so well for you,'
Jude said sincerely. 'And if it helps you kick the stress
you've been under, that can only benefit you and your
daughter in the long run.'

'I intend to throw out all my cigarettes.' Lauren's chin
came up in a determined little thrust. 'I'm going cold
turkey. If that's all right with you?'

'That's rather drastic.' Jude was cautious. 'Realise
you're probably going to feel you're being held together
by a few bits of string for a while. But if you think you
can handle it…'

'I can and I will.' Lauren pleated a strand of fair hair
around her finger. 'For Tally's sake I *have* to.'

'I admire your courage.' Jude sat back in his chair,

propping his fingers under his chin. 'You don't want to try the nicotine patches?'

'No.' Lauren was definite. 'I just want the poisonous stuff out of my system. I hope I won't start craving chocolates and stuff, though.'

'As an alternative, try to keep some vegetable sticks or plain popcorn handy,' Jude suggested. 'And if you normally have a smoke when you're on the phone, grab a pen and scribble block instead and doodle like mad.' He dug out a booklet from under a pile of paperwork and handed it to her. 'This should answer most of your questions. If not, bug me. I don't mind.'

Lauren raised softly shaded brows in query. 'You mentioned something about a course of relaxation exercises for me. Will that help?'

'If you're conscientious about it, yes, it will help tremendously.'

'All right.' She drew a deep breath. 'Where will I have to go—or will you—?'

'No,' he cut in with a smile. 'I'll refer you to Miriam Aldermann. She's a new physiotherapist in town. I've had a chat to her about Tally as well. She's agreed to treat both of you.'

The young mother's brows knitted together in sudden concern. 'Will it be expensive? At present, Tally's treatment at the hospital is free. I don't know whether I can afford a private physio, Dr Christie.'

'Miriam bulk-bills her patients, Lauren. Which means you don't need to pay anything up front. Your Medicare claim will cover the costs. Now, want to hear what I have in mind for your daughter?'

'Something new?'

'Yes.' Jude placed his hands palms down on the desk in front of him. 'I'd like to enrol Tally in an asthma trial study being conducted by the Jarvis Institute in Sydney. It's a highly reputable medical research unit headed by a thoracic physician, Jenna King.'

Lauren's gaze was suddenly uncertain. 'Does that mean I'd have to take Tally to Sydney?'

'Not initially, no.' Jude pulled a sheaf of notes towards him, scanned the top sheet for a moment and then looked up. 'Everything we need to do for Tally is here, and as her GP I'll liaise with Dr King. But naturally I'll need your permission for Tally to take part in the trial.'

'It won't be painful for her or anything, will it?'

'Absolutely not.' Jude's response was swift. 'The principle of the theory is that by learning to breathe differently, asthmatics may be able to reduce the severity of their disease and, in the long run, reduce their medication. Basically, it's recognising the symptoms of an attack and taking control. Tally will learn a technique of rebreathing.'

'That would be so wonderful... If she could be well...'

'Tally deserves every chance to have a normal active lifestyle,' Jude agreed. 'But we have to be realistic. There is still a long way to go with asthma research.'

'I'm aware of that,' Lauren said huskily. 'So, Doctor, what do we do now?'

'Well, first things first.' Jude leaned back and folded his arms. 'Tally has stabilised quite nicely, so I'm releasing her from hospital this afternoon. Will you be able to collect her?'

'Yes. It's my day off. And I'll be giving in my notice at the roadhouse tomorrow,' Lauren said happily. 'I'm looking forward to having much more quality time with my daughter.'

Jude nodded in satisfaction. It looked as if the Muir

ladies were on their way. 'We'll get together with Miriam quite soon,' he promised. 'I imagine she'll want you to sit in with Tally while she learns the new breathing techniques.'

'It sounds quite a lot to take in.' Lauren nibbled on her bottom lip. 'Will we get some kind of notes?'

'Better than that. Tally will be given a video explaining the exercises so you can view it at home together and then follow through. And I believe there's a diary as well. She'll be asked to record how she's feeling each day, any symptoms and so on, and whether she's had to use her medication.'

'It sounds like it's going to take up quite a lot of our time.' Looking thoughtful, Lauren touched the small medallion at her throat. 'But I really feel like we're getting somewhere at last. I'm so grateful to you for…well, for everything.'

'Tally's a great kid.' Jude shrugged a bit awkwardly. 'Let's just hope for a positive outcome for her, shall we?'

'So that's what I've arranged for the Muir family,' Jude concluded. It was near the end of their staff meeting and he looked expectantly between Kellah and Tony.

'Sounds like community medicine working to its full potential,' Tony approved. 'Excellent outcome, Jude.'

Kellah looked doubtful. 'You're sure it's a good idea for Lauren to quit without nicotine replacement therapy?'

'Well, I wouldn't recommend it for everyone,' Jude allowed. 'But Lauren seems quietly determined about this, and medically I didn't find anything untoward. So, for the moment I'm happy to let her run with it. She's agreed to some relaxation therapy but I'll certainly be keeping an eye on her over the next little while.'

'Fair enough.' Tony looked up over the top of his glasses. 'We'll support your decision any way we can. Right, Kellah?'

'Yes, of course.' She looked fleetingly at Jude and then away. 'Oh, by the way, I have an update on Leo. According to Bettina, he's responding to treatment exceptionally well so they've high hopes of still being able to go on their cruise.'

Tony scraped a hand around his jaw. 'It's one of those luxury liners so I imagine there'll be a full complement of medical and ancillary staff on board.'

'I'm sure Leo will be sensible enough not to jeopardise his recovery.' Jude flipped his pen back and forth between his fingers. 'I couldn't believe the positive change in his outlook when I saw him this morning.'

'That was more or less what Bettina told me as well,' Kellah said quietly. In fact, Leo's wife had had a lot more to say, telling Kellah that as a result of his heart attack Leo had begun to understand far more clearly his wife's need to be treated as normally as possible now her cancer was in remission.

'We held hands and talked for hours,' she'd told Kellah happily. 'Well, probably not hours.' She'd laughed on reflection. 'But just by holding hands, it was as though we were fusing our spirits into each other— drawing strength from each other. Does that sound fanciful?'

'Not at all, Bettina.' Kellah had choked back the sudden lump in her throat. 'I'm so glad you and Leo are back on the same wavelength again.'

Just recalling the conversation made Kellah blink a bit before she said, 'I had a word with the charge as well.

Apparently our Leo is facing up to his rehab with dogged determination.'

'Frightening to think he had to have a heart attack to knock some sense into him, though,' Tony mused gruffly. 'Well, if that's all, folks, I'm out of here. See you both tomorrow.'

''Night,' they chorused.

Tony was barely out the door when Kellah pushed her chair back awkwardly and whirled to her feet.

Jude's dark head snapped back in query. 'Where are you rushing off to?'

'I'm going home, Jude.' Kellah swallowed uncomfortably. 'In case you hadn't noticed, these daily meetings are extending our working day even further.'

'Don't gripe. You agreed they'd be useful.'

Goaded, she brought her chin up. She hadn't agreed to anything. He and Tony had set it up and she'd gone along with it for the sake of team harmony.

'So, tell me what else is eating you?' he insisted with a slightly grim smile.

'Nothing. I'm tired, that's all.'

He looked at her for a long moment, his expression unreadable. 'Let me spoil you, then. Come home with me. I'll cook for you.'

She was tempted. Lord, how she was tempted. But she shook her head. 'No, Jude, I don't think so.'

'Why not?' He waited, clearly expecting more.

Why not? Kellah swallowed the lump in her throat and sank back into her chair. She was attracted to Jude yet afraid to get too close to him. It wasn't what he wanted anyhow. He was blowing hot and cold, running scared. She knew the signs. And she certainly wasn't going to set herself up to be hurt.

His brows flexed. 'You're afraid you won't like my cooking.'

'Of course not.' She managed a strained little smile. 'You're…rushing me.' It was all she could think of to say.

'I'm offering to cook for you, nothing else.'

And if she believed that, she'd believe anything. Oh, certainly, it might be his intention now. But once they were alone in his house, caught up together over the intimacy of a shared meal and other things…

Perhaps out at Logger's Bend where he lived it would be cool enough to have a fire… Her mind ran ahead and she imagined the scene. She lowered her gaze. 'Um…rain-check?' she compromised.

'Rain-check,' he agreed easily. 'Saturday?'

Kellah felt her heart go into free-fall, her throat so dry she could hardly speak. 'You're determined about this, aren't you?' she said huskily, the sweet sting of anticipation already slithering up her spine.

'If you're free and I'm free,' he drawled, 'why not?'

Why not, indeed? She picked up several files and held them against her chest. 'I'm almost certain I'm babysitting for Jilly next Saturday. What about the following one?'

'OK.' Jude decided to quit while he was ahead. He spun his hands up behind his neck. 'Be prepared to make a day of it, hmm?' He sent her a smile that curled her toes. 'That'll give us a chance to have a tramp around the farm.'

'Farm?' Kellah couldn't help the teasing smile that curved her lips. 'I though it was a few acres.'

'To me it's a farm. It's got history,' he justified. 'And an old dairy. And you're laughing at me,' he accused, a reciprocal amusement stirring in his blue eyes.

'Never,' she assured him with a cheeky grin. 'I'll wear my farm clothes.'

'Do that.' He drew in his legs about to stand. 'And I'll wear mine.'

Had he been right to push her? Jude wrestled with the question all the way home. The invitation had surprised him as much as it had obviously disconcerted her. But she *had* accepted finally. And in the long run wasn't that all that mattered?

He gunned his car along the straight stretch of country road. For the first time in a long time, he was looking forward instead of backward.

What on earth had possessed her to agree? Kellah felt her stomach twist and knot at the prospect of spending the greater part of a Saturday with Jude.

Perhaps Jilly would have an emergency and need her to mind the children again and she could renege on Jude's invitation quite legitimately. She thrust the thought away, deeming it unworthy and a spineless cop-out.

Turning into her driveway, she faced the facts. She wanted to spend time with him. Needed to, if she was being totally honest. She felt alive in his company, all her senses singing. She even liked the way they sparred with one another, feeling her perceptions heighten as they hadn't for the longest time.

Nosing her car into the garage, she cut the engine. Was she halfway to falling in love with him?

CHAPTER SEVEN

'I'M GOING to change your medication back, Florence.' Kellah replaced the sphygmomanometer in its case and looked across at her elderly patient. Florence Tilley suffered from high blood pressure.

'That would relieve my mind, Dr Beaumont.' Florence rolled down the sleeve of her blouse and re-buttoned it at the wrist. 'I felt quite dizzy on those other tablets.'

'Well, they're relatively new and were worth a try.' Kellah tapped a few keys on her computer and printed out the prescription. 'Several of our patients were pleased with the results but obviously they don't suit you nearly as well as the original medication we started you on.'

Florence took the replacement prescription and tucked it into her handbag. 'Thank you, Doctor.'

'You're welcome, Florence. Don't forget to dispose of the other tablets, will you?'

'Yes, I'll do that. Thank you for reminding me, dear.'

'Now, anything I can do for Avril today?' Kellah smiled across to where Florence's elder sister sat, quietly singing to herself. Two years ago, she'd been diagnosed with Alzheimer's disease.

'She's pretty well at the moment.' Florence shrugged back into her cardigan. 'And she's happy at Rosewood with me.'

Kellah had visited the sisters at their rambling old farmhouse on numerous occasions. Now, of course, much of their land had been sold off and it was just the homestead standing in its mish-mash of fruit trees and overgrown flower-beds.

Kellah frowned slightly. Neither of the sisters was young any more but so far Florence seemed to be managing the care of her sister. Even though the onset of Alzheimer's had been a shock to them, Avril had retained her sweet nature but now depended on Florence for everything.

Recently, Kellah had gently canvassed the possibility of home help but Florence would have none of it. 'Avril feels safe with just the two of us,' she'd explained. 'And with you, of course, because she knows you mean her no harm. But I think a stranger about the place would upset her.'

Kellah had to be content with that but resolved to keep an eye on the situation at Rosewood. Now, she watched as Florence touched her sister on the shoulder and helped her up from the chair.

'Come along, Sissy. We're ready to go now.'

'Shall we get a sundae before we go home, Flo?' Avril's face held the innocent expectation of a child as she took her sister's arm.

'We usually do, don't we, pet?' Florence looked back, meeting Kellah's gaze above her sister's head

Kellah nodded. 'Ring me any time, day or night,' she said softly, and held the door open for them.

The Tilly sisters had been her last appointment and Kellah could hardly believe another Friday had come round so quickly. In her experience, time seem to drag when you had something to look forward to.

She gave an inward sigh. Was she really looking forward to spending tomorrow at Jude's farm? Almost absently, she began putting things to rights on her desktop.

What she was contemplating seemed like a giant step into the unknown.

But wasn't the beginning of any relationship like that? Except she had no real idea what Jude wanted, doubted if he knew himself. When she thought about it rationally, she guessed their involvement resembled some kind of awkwardly written script that neither of them knew how to follow.

Except for the chemistry between them, of course. That had left no room for doubt. She tried to ignore the candle-flicker of hope in her heart. So, they fancied one another. That was still light years away from a commitment. Even thinking about that made her nerve-ends tingle as though they were attached to a thousand fine wires.

Crossing to the recessed wardrobe, she opened the door and slid her linen jacket from its hanger. As she shrugged it on, she remembered with relief that yesterday they'd decided there was no more need for their daily meetings after surgery. They would now return to getting together on a weekly basis.

She took her medical case from its locker and thought how good it would be to get home. Casting an all-encompassing look around her room, she checked everything was in order—blinds closed, computer shut down, files locked away.

She turned at the sharp rat-a-tat on her door. 'Come in.'

Jude poked his head in. 'Just off?'

She nodded, moistening her lips, suddenly, unaccountably nervous.

'Thought we'd better make arrangements for tomorrow.' His dark brows rose in query as he came in and shut the door. 'Still coming?'

Kellah's heart thumped. 'If I'm still invited.'

He gave a theatrical sigh. 'What do you think?' Parking himself on the corner of her desk, he raised his arms, pressing the heels of his hands against his eyes. 'Lord, I'll be glad to see the back of this week.'

'It has been a bit frantic,' she agreed, looking covertly at him. He needed to relax and for a split second she contemplated how she could make that happen… 'Are you going to give me directions to your place?' She heard her voice over-bright and clawed back her wayward thoughts.

'Don't be nuts.' He scoffed at the idea. 'I'll come and collect you.'

Kellah looked alarmed. 'I'd rather bring my own car, if you don't mind.'

'Why?'

'Because,' she said inadequately.

'Kellah, I'm not about to stalk you,' he said, his gaze full of reproach. 'Can't we look at tomorrow as a chance to get to know one another away from the surgery?'

She hadn't thought of it like that. Her sudden smile was tremulous and etched with relief. 'I'd like that.'

Jude turned slightly, lifting his hand and bringing it to her face. He cupped her cheek, brushing his thumb along the side of her jaw. 'That's the first halfway decent smile you've given me, do you know that? What time shall I pick you up tomorrow?' he tacked on gruffly.

'Not before two.' She edged away from his touch, her breath jamming. 'I've stuff to do around the house first.'

'OK.' He gave a half-smile, raising both hands in capitulation. 'I want to check on a couple of patients at the hospital so I'll do that before I collect you. Then, with a bit of luck, we'll have the rest of the day to ourselves.'

*   *   *

What should she wear? Kellah sifted through the possibilities and sighed. Why on earth was she getting into a tizz? They'd be out in the bush, not in some glamorous restaurant. Nevertheless, a faint excitement began to build in her stomach as she thought of spending the afternoon with Jude.

She was ready and waiting for him when he rang her doorbell and less than five minutes later they were on their way to his property, Karingal.

'It's an indigenous name for "happy home",' he explained, as they drove. 'I've boned up a bit on the history of the house, too. Apparently, it was built in the 1930s.'

'Way back then?' A slight frown touched Kellah's forehead. 'Are you sure it's not built over an old coal mine?'

Jude gave her a sharp glance. 'Surely that would have shown up on the title deed?'

'Well, one would hope so,' Kellah rejoined thoughtfully.

A beat of silence.

'You're taking the mick, aren't you?' Jude's look was decidedly wry.

She chuckled. 'Had you going there, didn't I?'

'Mmm. I can see I'll have to think of a suitable payback,' he drawled, his eyes flickering to hers, the warmth in them sending a soft wash of colour over her cheeks.

'This part here is a fauna reserve,' Jude pointed out a bit later as they drove through the farm gates and onto his property.

Kellah craned closer to the window. 'So you have bird and animal watchers here on a regular basis?'

He shrugged. 'I believe so. They don't bother me. And here's the house,' he tacked on softly, as they crested the hill to reveal the simple skillion-roofed structure.

'It was advertised as a "renovator's dream".' He raised a dark brow expressively. 'And I guess most people would have put a bulldozer through it, but at the time I needed something to keep me physically occupied and it fitted the bill perfectly. And you must admit it has a great roofline to it,' he suggested hopefully.

'I think it's perfect.' Kellah's voice was hushed. 'I can't wait to see inside.'

A few minutes later, she was saying, 'What's this, Jude?' Entranced, she touched her hand to the ornately carved piece in the lounge room.

Jude looped his arm casually about her shoulders and sent her an indulgent smile. 'It's a Javanese dowry chest. I picked it up at an auction.'

'I've never been to an auction. It must be fun.'

His mouth puckered briefly. 'Sometimes. It can also be a bit fierce, when several bidders are after the same item.'

'Well, you must have outbid them all to get this beauty,' she rejoined, her eyes alight with interest as she turned aside to explore the intricately patterned doors of the chest.

'Next time there's an auction on locally, I'll take you,' he promised. 'The clearing-out sales at the old homesteads are the best.'

'You're on.' An expectant smile curved her lips, her eyes continuing to explore the room, registering the ancient fireplace and the scattering of family photographs on the mantelpiece.

'Like to see the rest now?' Jude took her hand and she felt the warm slide of his thumb across her knuckles before his palm totally engulfed them.

Nearly every room in the house looked out onto the

verandah or garden. 'There seem so many nooks and crannies—I just love it.'

Jude was clearly delighted with her reaction. 'I took a few months off to work on it. Don't go imagining I'm filthy rich, though.' He held up a hand as if to emphasise the point. 'I'd managed to save a bit and a legacy from my grandmother helped no end.'

She made a face at him. 'The way you talked, I imagined the place wasn't far short of falling down. Oh, boy…' She paused at the next doorway and looked in. 'This kitchen is serious work space. Even Jilly would approve. Where on earth did you get that bench?'

'It's as solid as it looks, too.' Jude drew her close to his side, guiding her through the doorway for a better look. 'It's an original. Came out of a draper's shop. Remember the good old days, when they used to throw down those huge bolts of material and measure out the yardage for the customers?'

'Just.' Deliciously aware of the warmth of his touch, Kellah tinkled a laugh. 'And it's *metres* now,' she reminded him. 'So, what about all this stainless-steel shelving? Did you do that yourself?'

'It wasn't too difficult. I got it pre-cut at the local hardware store. All in all I achieved maximum kitchen for minimum dollars. Now the bedrooms.' He flashed her a grin, his fingers tightening. 'Interested?'

Of course she was interested. Just the thought of bedrooms in connection with Jude had her pulses racing.

But his manner was very laid-back as he opened the doors on two smallish bedrooms, one of which he was obviously using as an office, and then proceeded to the main one at the front of the house.

It was heaven. And what Kellah would have chosen herself, given the space and the layout of the house. The floor was carpeted in softest grey, the walls a deep muted blue and the windows had plain linen blinds which were presently pulled up to allow the light in. Her mouth dried as she looked at the beautiful bed. 'It's cherry wood, isn't it?' She moved in front of him, touching a hand to the curved bed end.

'Yes, it is.' He seemed surprised at her knowledge of the old-fashioned timber. 'I love its warmth, don't you?'

Her heart lurched and she sidetracked quickly. 'Unusual shape.'

'It is,' he acknowledged gravely. 'It's called a sleigh bed.'

Kellah had a quick mental picture of a sleigh on runners drawn by horses or huskies across the snow and thought what a romantic concept it was for the design for a bed.

'I always wanted one,' he confessed rather sheepishly. 'Ever since I saw the style in an American magazine. I had it custom-made.'

'For a moment I thought you were going to say you'd made it yourself,' Kellah teased, lifting her gaze to the window and looking out to the valley beyond. For a moment the silence was absolute. 'All this is a credit to you, Jude,' she complimented him.

He shrugged slightly. 'There's a lot of satisfaction in working with your hands and I enjoy the buzz of actually seeing a project come to fruition.'

'So, how come you became a doctor and not a carpenter?'

'Always wanted to, I guess. You?'

'Pretty much. But, being raised on a farm, I was possibly drawn more to vet science.'

'And that wasn't an option?'

She made an ambiguous little moue and shrugged. 'In

my last year at high school I did work experience with the local vet. When I saw what he had to do, and the gear he had to do it with, I kind of went off the idea.'

Jude's eyes crinkled, as he grinned. 'And people medicine seemed a far better career.'

'I guess so…'

A gossamer-thin thread of awareness seemed to shimmer between them, drawing them slowly together. And quite without thinking, because it suddenly seemed the most natural thing in the world, Kellah took the initiative, tightening her fingers in his and feeling him respond.

'Show me over the farm,' she invited softly.

They went outside.

'We can go on the trail bikes or we can walk,' Jude said.

'Oh, let's walk.' Kellah tossed him a quick smile. 'Except for a couple of hospital visits, I hardly got out of the surgery this week.'

It was an exhilarating and easy walk along the track through the valley, the air almost bitingly crisp. Hand in hand, they crossed a stream and kept walking, up steep terrain now, to the highest point of Jude's land.

'This is as far as we go.' He stopped and wheeled her round, linking his arms about her from behind. 'Pretty special, isn't it?'

'Oh, yes…' Eyes half-closed, Kellah placed her hands on his forearms, almost absently stroking her fingers over the fine olive texture of his skin. The view to the valley and beyond was never-ending, hazed in the soft blue-grey of afternoon. And the air was still. So still.

'What a view…' Kellah tipped her head back to look at him. 'Makes you feel so good to be alive, doesn't it?'

'That—and being with someone special,' Jude added, a throaty edge to his voice.

She shivered faintly. *If he doesn't kiss me, then I'll jolly well kiss him,* she thought desperately, and turned in his arms.

He leant into her, raising the cascade of hair where it fell over her shoulders, exposing the side of her throat. Kellah felt his breath warm against her skin and then came the light rasp of his tongue.

'Jude…' She gusted his name on a shaken breath and sighed in rapture when his mouth felt its way to the corner of hers.

'This feels like magic,' she whispered hazily when his mouth lifted.

'And you're lovely…' It was like a groan. Gathering her in, he teased her mouth open, drinking the taste of her as though he might quench the thirst of a lifetime.

And she responded, shifting against him, taking him to her. Her hands travelled in a hard sweep under his T-shirt, her fingers making a hungry exploration of the ridge of his spine, his shoulder blades and running higher to stroke the sinewy muscles at his nape.

Jude made a muted sound in his throat. It was like the growl of a lion, shuddering through his whole length. His hands came down to bracket her hips, then drift lower to cup her behind through the cotton fabric of her trousers, then climb upwards to the strip of bare skin at her waist.

'Don't stop…' she murmured against his mouth, her skin prickling beneath the teasing caress of his palm.

He pulled back, as if he'd been stung, grabbing her hands to still them.

Faint shock widened her eyes. 'Jude?'

'It's OK…' He held her closely, pressing kisses

against her temple as if she were a child who had to be soothed. Then he pulled away, his chest lifting in a huge controlling breath. 'Let's sit for a while.' Sliding his arm around her waist, he guided her across to a leopard tree and a dappled patch of shade beneath.

For a long time they did little else than absorb their surroundings, the strobes of sunlight dipping deep into the valley below, the pungent scent of eucalypts and early wattle.

'Sometimes I wish Dad and Mum hadn't sold our farm,' she mused.

'Well, they must have had their reasons.' In a skilful rearrangement of muscles, Jude eased her back against him, his arms forming a cradle for her slender body.

'Oh, I can see it from their point of view.' With a feeling of rightness, Kellah curled her body into his, each curve and hollow finding a home, a placement, as though they'd been specially carved for each other.

'Dad had reached sixty and was obviously slowing down a bit,' she said softly. 'And farming these days is very labour-intensive.'

'And it wasn't as though you or your sister had any desire to farm, was it?'

'Odd that, isn't it?'

'Perhaps, not,' Jude considered, overlapping his hands around her waist. He nuzzled a kiss into her hair. 'Sometimes a family tradition skips a generation. It might turn out *your* children will want to pursue a life on the land.'

Kellah turned and smiled up at him. 'What a nice thought.' They were silent then, until she said tentatively, 'You mentioned you'd bought Karingal a couple of years ago, when you were here, visiting Sarah. Did you always mean to settle here eventually?'

She felt him tense. 'Possibly... I'd been overseas,

working for one of the care agencies.' He paused and cleared his throat. 'A lot had happened. When I came to Sarah's I was an emotional mess…'

The scenario he painted rocked a terrible uneasiness into the pit of Kellah's stomach. Her heart began thudding heavily. Oh, lord. Was he waiting for her to press him further? Throw him an emotional lifeline of some kind? 'Are you OK now?' She raced in quickly with the question before she could lose her nerve.

'Yes… No… I honestly don't know.' The ambiguity of his words was reflected in his expression because he suddenly looked very uncertain.

'Jude…' Kellah gnawed at her bottom lip. Should she press him further and risk the possibility of him shutting down again?

'I know what you're asking, Kellah,' he said roughly.

'For your sake, not for mine,' she said pointedly. 'And only if you want to.'

He was silent for a long time. Then he expelled a harsh breath and turned his head towards her. His mouth lifted in a token smile. 'I guess I'm never going to get a better offer.'

His small attempt at humour touched her and she held out a hand to him.

He took it, pressing her fingers tightly as if to gain strength from the contact. There was silence again as if he was searching for the right words and then he began to talk very quietly and measuredly.

'When I came to Chadwick, Sarah suggested I needed a purpose, a reason to stay. She mentioned putting down roots or something similar. So, after a huge bout of indecision, I bought the house, worked some of the angst out of my system and then went back overseas.'

'Where were you stationed?'

He hesitated infinitesimally. 'Qandahar, in Afghanistan. The situation was volatile—lots of skirmishes with the rebels. Sometimes we had to bribe people to get out of the camp to go to the village and bribe them again to get back in. Getting our medical supplies through was a nightmare…'

Kellah gave a sharp glance at the sudden tight set of his neck and shoulders. 'So why did you want to go back?'

How on earth did he answer that? Jude eased his head back against the trunk of the tree, unaware his eyes had assumed a bleak look. He clamped his jaw and agonised whether now was the time to tell her everything, but his gut did a somersault at the thought of resurrecting it all.

He rubbed a hand across his forehead, feeling the familiar tightening in his throat, but something compelled him to plough on. 'Angela and I were instrumental in establishing the hospital. I wanted to go back and see how everyone was coping.'

Angela? Kellah's breathing faltered and almost stopped. Why did she know instantly they'd reached the crux of his vacillating behaviour? She continued to sit there, her fingers tightly interlinked with his, the implication of his words going round and round in her head. She took a breath so deep it hurt. 'So, who's Angela? A colleague?'

'Much more.' Jude closed his eyes momentarily. 'She was my medical partner, my friend—my lover. And she was killed,' he added harshly. 'Needlessly cut down by a land mine.

'We were in a Jeep together, travelling back to camp from the village. I was driving and we had a child with us. It all happened in a split second. The passenger side caught most of the impact from the blast. Angie threw herself across the boy. He survived...' He stopped and rubbed a hand across his eyes. 'As I did.'

His voice had sounded harsh and scrappy and Kellah bit her lips tightly together and shook her head. Even a first-year psychology student would have diagnosed Jude was suffering from survivor's guilt. Nowadays it was a recognised syndrome, like PTSD—post-traumatic stress disorder.

Oh, Jude. Wordlessly, she reached out and wrapped her arms around him.

'Damn,' he whispered, and turned his face away, fighting his feelings.

Much later, Jude hauled them upright and silently and slowly they made their way home. Dusk was falling. It would be winter quite soon, Kellah thought, hugging her arms around herself instinctively.

'Would you like to borrow a sweater?' Jude had seen her action.

'I'll be fine once we get inside.' She went ahead of him up the shallow back steps, through the laundry and into the kitchen. 'I'll, um, freshen up and then I'll give you a hand with dinner.' She smiled faintly. 'What are we having, by the way?'

'Ah...' Jude made a supreme effort to concentrate. 'Lamb ragout. I made it last night. It's always better for the keeping. Do you remember where the bathroom is? Along the hall to your left.'

Kellah nodded but still hesitated. 'Jude...I have to say this. I can't imagine what you've been through but I feel your grief...' Her breath caught and shuddered in her throat.

'Thank you.' The words escaped mechanically from his lips.

'And I won't insult you by offering platitudes and suggesting you move on. But perhaps you should think about some counselling.'

His head came up as if she'd slapped him. 'I've had counselling,' he said in a cool, quiet voice. 'Look, I'm sorry…' Lifting his hands, he scrubbed them back through his hair. 'I didn't mean to lumber you with any of this.'

'You haven't.' She watched him as he turned towards the fridge, pulling the door open and staring blindly inside. Oh, lord. Her hand went to her throat, the emotion of the moment overwhelming her like a tide. Hardly realising what she was doing, she took the couple of steps necessary and peered over his shoulder. 'Aha!' She strove for a joking quality in her voice, reaching inside and pulling out the dark blue casserole dish. 'Is this perchance what you're looking for, Doctor?'

Turning, she moved past him and placed the ovenware on the counter top. With a little flourish, she took off the lid and wrinkled her nose. 'I was expecting gourmet. This looks like a glorified stew.'

Jude's grin was barely there but what there was shone like sunshine breaking through cloud. 'Get out of here!'

Kellah turned on the tap and, cupping her hands, bent over the basin, splashing cold water on to her face over and over again. Straightening, she regarded her reflection in the mirror above the basin. She'd certainly had better days. Her intake of breath was almost audible.

What on earth am I doing here?

Almost mechanically, she plucked a towel from its rail and began to pat her skin dry. Since the first time she'd met him, Jude had filled her thoughts. And she'd been so wrong about him. She shook her head in disbelief.

His teasing manner that had so unsettled her in the beginning had been sheer bravado—an act to hide his pain.

Oh, help. Blinking quickly, she replaced the towel carefully on its rail and bit her lip. She *loved* him. In the same second she snapped that part of her mind closed with the gut-wrenching realisation of what that meant.

How could she even think of a future with Jude when he was still so bound up with the past?

CHAPTER EIGHT

HE'D probably stuffed everything up. Almost savagely, Jude grabbed several lemons from the fruit basket and began cutting them into wedges to serve with his ragout.

Why on earth would Kellah want to be bothered with him now? For crying out loud, *no one* in their right mind would want to get involved with him and his stockpile of emotional baggage.

And yet lately he'd found the weight lifting in odd indefinable ways. He'd actually had days when he hadn't thought of Angie—and then felt guilty. He blew out a long breath and crossed to the stove.

Was Kellah right? Perhaps he did need more counselling.

With a snort of self-disgust, he began feeding lengths of pasta into the rapidly boiling water.

Kellah made herself take several deep, controlling breaths before returning to the kitchen. 'You seem to have everything under control.' Crossing to the bench, she watched him at work. He was truly at home in his kitchen.

'This won't take long.' He looked up, his mouth a bit tight as he smiled. 'We've time for a drink. I've still some of the Merlot left from the ragout. Suit you?'

'Nicely, thanks.'

'I've lit the fire in the lounge.' He spun round, collecting the wine and a couple of glasses, and headed for the door.

She followed him through to the cosily fitted-out

room, taking her time to absorb its atmosphere. Apart from the Javanese chest, it was simply furnished with a rug in natural colours on the polished floorboards, a long sofa in front of the fireplace. Taking her wine, she wandered over to take a closer look at the collection of photographs on the mantlepiece.

They were obviously family pictures—but maybe not this one. It was a snapshot in black and white of a small boy, about seven or eight she judged. His hair was coal-black and he held his head at an angle, his gaze wide and trusting, the beginnings of a tentative smile on his face. Kellah ran a fingertip over the frame.

'That's Kamal,' Jude said quietly from behind her.

She lifted her glass and took a mouthful of her wine, hoping he would fill her in but he didn't. The silence was gentle, though, and there was warmth in Jude's gaze. She plucked up her courage. 'He's a handsome little boy.'

'Yes.' Jude picked up the photo, studied it for a moment and put it back. 'Angela and I were going to adopt him.'

Kellah saw the heart-breaking sadness that froze his features for an instant and another cog fell into place—the reason for his white-hot anger against what he saw as others' prejudices about overseas adoption.

'I'm sorry,' she murmured, knowing it was inadequate, but she didn't know what else to say. She guessed if he wanted to tell her more, he would. It seemed he did.

'Sit down for a minute.' He placed a guiding hand at her nape and led her back to the sofa. 'I'd like to tell you about him.' He glanced at his watch and frowned. 'Perhaps I'd better check the pasta first. Won't be a tick,' he promised, his long legs carrying him from the room in a couple of strides.

Kellah had almost finished her wine when he returned.

'Everything's on hold,' he said with a crooked smile and took his place beside her on the sofa. Taking her glass, he topped it up and slid it across to her, careful not to touch her.

'We met Kamal in the market,' he began. 'He was barely eight years old, working as a shoe shine boy. He worked all day, every day for about seventy cents in our currency.

'Whenever Angie and I saw him, he'd call out, "*A salaam va laikum*", which means, the peace of God be upon you. For a little lad, he had such dignity.' Jude leaned forward, rotating his glass between the palms of his hands.

'We decided to find out about him. It took ages but finally we tracked him to an orphanage. His family had been wiped out due to the war. Our Kamal was the only one remaining.'

'After a lot of red tape, we finally got permission to take him out on our days off and gradually got to know him.' Jude took a hard breath and let it go. 'The idea to try to adopt him began from a nebulous kind of conversation one night and then next day Angie asked me if I'd meant it.' His smile was fleeting. 'The upshot was we began enquiring what we had to do—if it was even possible.'

'And it was?'

There was a pause while Jude studied the dusky red wine in his glass.

'Yes... But there was a stipulation.' His voice faltered. 'We had to be married.'

'I assumed you were.' Kellah's words were guarded.

He looked into the fire. 'It had never seemed necessary before. We were committed. A piece of paper would have added nothing to our relationship.'

'Except legality.'

He shrugged. 'We fully intended to get married some day. Probably when our tour of duty was finished. But just then it wasn't a priority.'

Until you wanted to adopt Kamal. But Kellah kept her thoughts to herself.

There was a short silence and then he said starkly, 'We were in the process of getting our paperwork together, hoping like crazy a missionary would come through to perform the ceremony. But we waited too long…'

'Oh, Jude…'

In the end, Kellah didn't know who was holding who the tightest. She only knew right at that moment she didn't want to be anywhere else.

Eventually, they stirred, and began moving quietly and gently through the rest of the evening. Kellah found some plain white candles that he was obviously keeping in the event of a power cut. She lit several and dotted them about the lounge room—not knowing quite why she was doing it.

Jude said the pasta was done for and offered to make a fresh lot, but Kellah vetoed that so they dished up the food and ate off trays in front of the fire. A shower of rain fell and the night drew in around them.

'Ready for coffee now?' Kellah swung upright. 'Stay there, I'll make it.'

'No, you're my guest,' Jude insisted. 'I'll get it.'

In the end they both went through to the kitchen.

Watching him spoon coffee into the mugs, Kellah said, 'Dinner was lovely, Jude.'

His lopsided smile was edged with vulnerability. 'Despite the pasta tasting like old rope?'

She wrinkled her nose at him. 'What's a bit of old rope between friends?'

Almost as if he'd suddenly made up his mind about something, Jude turned to her, spreading his hands over her shoulders and looking deeply into her eyes. 'You're a helluva listener, Kellah Beaumont,' he said, his voice rough and not quite even.

They were halfway through their coffee when she said quietly, 'So, do you still keep in touch with Kamal?'

'Yes.' Jude's face lit up. 'I write and he sends me funny little letters in return. He's learning English. And I send money so he doesn't have to work any more.'

Kellah shook her head silently. How could anyone live their life so drenched in emotion? She doubted she could. She wondered if Jude felt better for having told her his most private memories. She hoped so.

It was late and the fire had all but gone out. Jude roused himself, unwinding off the sofa and taking her with him. He looked deep into her eyes and very lightly traced the contour of her lips with his index finger. 'It's time I took you home,' he said, before bending to her and touching her mouth with his.

Kellah shut her eyes, parted her lips and drank him in.

Preoccupied as they were, it was several moments before they registered the banging on the front door.

'What in blazes—?' Jude broke away, moving quickly to investigate. Kellah followed, for some reason feeling a tug of unease as he threw open the door and activated the porch light.

A young man dressed in jeans, a bush shirt and muddy trainers rocked agitatedly from one foot to the other. At

Jude's appearance, he pulled back uncertainly. 'Are you a doctor, mate?'

'We both are.' Jude's response was clipped. He indicated Kellah who was peering over his shoulder. 'This is Kellah Beaumont and I'm Jude Christie. Has something happened?'

'My wife's having a baby.'

Jude looked blank. 'What, now?'

The young man nodded vigorously. 'Her waters have broken.' He took a deep breath. 'We're camped in the fauna reserve. We came to track the wombats. You have to do it at night.'

Kellah stepped forward into the light. 'When is your baby due, Mr...?'

'Phelan, Shane Phelan. My wife's Tracey. The baby's not due for two weeks.'

Which was neither here nor there, Kellah thought practically. Babies came when they were ready.

'I had to leave her and run up here.' Shane shot a hand distractedly through his hair. 'We don't have our car with us. We had someone drop us off—so we wouldn't disturb the wombats.'

Oh, good grief! Jude clamped down on his frustration. 'Have you rung for an ambulance, Shane?'

'No. Mobile's on the blink—or I couldn't get a signal. Someone said a doctor was living here so I figured you might help.'

Kellah turned to Jude and said quietly, 'I'll ring for an ambulance. But it's late and it's Saturday night. It could be a while. And if the waters have already broken...?'

They might have to deliver Tracey here. Jude was already tapping his pockets for his car keys. 'Shane.' He addressed the agitated father-to-be calmly. 'I'll get my

car out and we'll go and collect your wife. You'll have
to direct me to your camp.'

'I can do that, Doc.' He seemed pathetically grateful.
'We'll take her straight to the hospital, yeah?'

'Perhaps not.' Jude was cautious. 'I'll know more
when I've examined her. If there's time, Tracey might
be more comfortable waiting here for the ambulance and
we can keep an eye on her. Is it your first baby?'

'Second.' Shane gulped. 'She was pretty quick with
the first.'

'I'll start getting things ready here in case.' Kellah's
tone was brisk. 'Call me on your mobile, Jude, and let
me know what's happening.'

'Will do.' He turned back into the hallway and collected a wind jacket from its hook and tugged it on.
'You'll find extra supplies in the top cupboard directly
opposite the desk in my office. There's even a maternity
pack, I think.'

'I'll improvise if not.' She shooed him off and then
set to work.

Without any history of Tracey's previous labour, Kellah knew she was guessing about what they might expect. And the ambulance could be anything up to an
hour, the base had said. She'd best prepare for the possibility of having to deliver the baby here.

They'd need somewhere warm. Tracey could be in a
right old state. In Kellah's experience, once their waters
had broken, many women were prone to a kind of de-
layed shock, shivering uncontrollably. So, even though
the fire was at the ember stage, she decided the lounge
room was the best option.

She began ticking off what they'd need in her head.
Thank goodness the sofa was one of the modern ones

that converted to a bed, she thought, tucking plastic bin liners over the firm square cushions.

Grabbing towels out of the linen closet, she sprinted to the laundry, throwing them into the dryer. At least they'd have something warm to wrap the baby in.

Then, carrying an armful of sheets, she tore back to the lounge. 'Oh, Jude, you sweet, old-fashioned guy,' she murmured, catching the soft drift of lavender as she unfurled them over the plastic liners and tucked them in.

Her spirits drooped slightly. The lavender was probably Sarah's doing. At the moment, Jude seemed to be depending on his sister for any feminine touches in his life. Now, what else? Combing her fingers back through her hair, Kellah locked them on top of her head, thinking. Medical supplies.

Hurrying through to Jude's office, she dragged a set of steps across to the wall of fitted cupboards and hoisted herself up. Good heavens! Her eyebrows peaked. He had a small emergency department in here. Selecting what they'd need, she climbed gingerly down from her perch and took her booty back to the lounge room.

Come on, Jude, get a move on and call me, she fretted. She tore open the maternity pack and spread out the contents.

Under Shane's directions, Jude was at the Phelan's camp-site within a few minutes. Pulling back the tent flap, he saw the young mother huddled on her side on top of a sleeping bag. She was keening softly, pulling her knees up as though she wanted to push.

In a couple of strides, he was beside her and hunkering down. 'Tracey,' he said gently, 'I'm Jude. I'm a doctor.'

'Oh-h…' Tracey bit her lips together and grimaced. 'Shane found you…'

'He certainly did. Now, I need to see what you're doing, all right? I'll be as gentle as I can.' Jude's examination was brief but thorough. He reckoned they had thirty minutes at the outside. He slung his stethoscope aside. He had no desire to deliver this baby by dodgy torchlight, although he'd done so many times in Qandahar. *Don't go there.* He clamped his jaw, dragging his thoughts back to the present.

'What do you think, Doctor?' Tracey looked at Jude with huge, frightened eyes.

'I think we'll get you straight up to my house, Tracey. This baby is not waiting.'

Tracey whimpered. 'Shane…?'

'I'm here, Trace.' Shane took his wife's hand and squeezed it hard. 'We shouldn't have come here this weekend,' he agonised. 'I'm an idiot!' He flung a desperate look at Jude. 'Is the baby all right?'

'As far as I can tell, your wife and baby are fine, Shane.' Jude drew himself upright. 'Now, I'm just going to step outside to call Dr Beaumont on my mobile. Then I'll need your help to get Tracey into the car.'

'She's almost fully dilated and the baby seems small,' Jude relayed to Kellah.

Kellah felt a lick of unease. 'We're not going to have a problem, are we?'

'Shouldn't think so. Foetal heartbeat is good and strong. Everything OK your end?'

'Yes, I've done the best I can. Are you on your way now?'

'Shouldn't be more than a few minutes.'

Kellah went to wash her hands and when the little party arrived, she took charge. 'I've set things up in the lounge. It's warm and there's a bit of space for us to work.'

'Good.' Jude carried their patient in and set her gently on the sofa-bed. 'Not long to go, I think,' he added, when Tracey moaned slightly.

'We don't have any history, so I'll get a line in, in case there's a bleed.' Kellah's fingers were quick and neat. 'Tracey, you're doing great,' she said. 'What are you hoping for?'

'Doesn't matter.' Tracey gasped. 'Oh, I want to push…'

'Not quite yet, honey.' Kellah brushed the damp hair off Tracey's brow. 'Shane.' She addressed the young husband who was looking rather helpless and over-whelmed. 'If you'd like to find the bathroom and wash your hands, you'll be able to cut your baby's cord, di-rectly.'

'Me?' He swallowed convulsively.

Jude grinned. 'Get a rattle on, mate. It's all about to happen.'

Kellah thought that she and Jude could have been practising medicine together for years so well did they co-ordinate their skills.

While she knelt at Tracey's side and helped her into position, Jude snapped on gloves and prepared to deliver the baby.

'Here we go, folks,' he said, cradling the infant's head in his hands. 'Gentle push, Tracey—well done. Rest a beat now and gently does it again—that's terrific.' Looking up, he encompassed them all with a smile of satisfaction. 'It's a wee girl and she's looking good.'

'Oh. We really wanted a girl.' Tracey was laughing and crying at the same time.

'A little sister for Tom.' Shane was beaming and clutching his wife's hand.

'Will you make a note of the time, please, Kellah?' Jude wondered why his eyes had suddenly gone all misty.

'Well done, you.' Kellah's glance at him was soft. 'That was a very smooth delivery.'

'Thank you both so much,' Tracey said shyly, her eyes filling as she looked down at her brand new daughter now snugly wrapped in a warm towel.

'She's lovely.' Kellah stroked a knuckle across the newborn's little cheek. 'Do you have a name for her?'

'Meryan,' Tracey said without hesitation. 'We'll call her Meri.'

'That's sweet.' Kellah blinked away the sudden cloudiness in her eyes. She cleared her throat. 'Jude's making a cup of tea. I'm sure we could all do with one.'

'Come on, let's get this lot cleared away.' Kellah was looking purposeful. The ambulance carrying the Phelan family had been and gone and she was feeling a terrible sense of anticlimax.

'Hell's teeth!' Jude surveyed the chaos in his lounge room and gave a short hollow laugh. 'Do you believe any of this actually happened?'

'Of course it did.' Kellah began stripping sheets off the sofa. 'There's a new little member of the human race to prove it.' She chuckled. 'Brings back memories of long nights in Obstetrics during rotation, doesn't it?'

Jude grunted a non-reply. The whole day had reminded him of many things. But certainly not that. 'Look, thanks, but that'll do for now, Kellah.' Unceremoniously, he plucked the bundle of soiled linen out of her arms and threw it aside. 'Now, if you'll get your gear together, I'll run you home.'

Kellah stopped as if she'd been struck. Her eyes widened and she sent him a doubtful, sideways look. 'Are you OK?'

'What does it look like?' He sounded tired and the eyes that lifted briefly to hers were guarded and shadowed.

Her heart bounced sickeningly. He'd spent most the day on an emotional roller-coaster, of course he wasn't OK. 'Look.' She spread her hands in appeal. 'You're tired. I'm sure you don't feel like turning out again to drive me home and then having to come all the way back.'

Jude swore under his breath. 'Kellah, just give me a bit of space here, OK?'

Was he insinuating she was intruding? Her eyes filled with reproach. 'I was merely suggesting I make up a bed in the spare room.'

The corners of his mouth tightened ominously.

'I'll get my things.' Feeling oddly chilled, Kellah went into the second bedroom where she'd left her small canvas backpack. And when she came back out, Jude had the engine running and the headlights were already shining down the track that led out of the property to the main road.

Peremptorily, he switched on the car radio and under the camouflage of a late-night programme of country music, they made their way back to town in awkward silence.

There was no point in inviting him inside, Kellah decided grimly as Jude slid the Audi to a stop outside her apartment building. She certainly wasn't going to set herself up for another rebuff.

With fingers that refused to co-operate, she finally managed to unfasten her seat belt. 'There's no need to get out,' she managed tightly.

'I'll see you safely to your door.' Jude released the locks and threw off his seat belt.

Simmering, she said, 'Really, I'll be fine. The sensor lights will automatically come on as soon as I walk up the path.'

'I'll walk you up.'

Kellah gritted her teeth and swung out of the car. In her agitation she dropped her keys on the porch and Jude, right behind her, picked them up.

Refusing to do anything so undignified as trying to wrestle them from him, she stood back and allowed him to open the door.

'I'll be fine now,' she said tersely.

'Kellah.' He snapped forward and took her by the shoulders. 'Look, I'm sorry I snarled at you earlier. It's nothing personal.'

Her throat lumped. 'You don't have to explain…'

'Yes, I do.' He looked as though it hurt him to breathe. 'I want you to know that today, with you, I reached a kind of watershed.'

Was that good or bad? Kellah took a ragged breath. 'I listened, Jude—that's all.'

'*That* was everything.'

Kellah licked her lips, her normal thought patterns jamming as he gently turned her face up towards him. He looked down at her for what seemed like an age before he gathered her in and gently kissed her mouth.

On a little sigh she opened to him, allowing her tongue to meet his—fleetingly, lightly, a butterfly's touch—and for a long moment they remained barely moving, their lips brushing, satin-soft, a rhapsody of the sweetest kind.

Finally, Jude drew back, and put her gently from him. 'I'll see you on Monday.' The brief feathering of his lips against her throat left fire.

A fire, Kellah realised dazedly, that if it wasn't quenched soon would roar out of control.

CHAPTER NINE

KELLAH arrived at the surgery early on Monday. But it seemed someone had got there earlier still. When she opened the door of her consulting room, she was met by the heady perfume of roses.

Oh, lord. She felt her heart flounder and her eyes prickled suddenly. They *had* to be from Jude. She bit her lip, wondering how he'd got in, and then remembered there was a master key for all the rooms.

And the roses were lovely—old-fashioned climbing ones, deepest cream edged with pink, a mix of big, fully-blown blooms intermingled with tiny perfect buds that would open in a day or so.

She touched a finger to the satin-smooth petals. She loved them.

'Oh, Kel. Good, you're in.' Teri popped her head around the door. 'Could you see an early bird?'

Flushing, Kellah jumped out of her daydream and looked round over her shoulder at the receptionist. 'Oh, hi, Teri. Come on in. I was just, uh, about to find a vase for these...'

'Roses?' Teri finished for her, dimpling a teasing smile. 'Aren't they gorgeous? And they've still got dew on them,' she marvelled, sticking her nose inside one particularly breath-taking bloom and sighing with ecstasy. 'Where did they come from?'

'Well, the garden, obviously,' Kellah flannelled, flushing a little more.

'*Your* garden? Oh, you lucky thing. I've only got rockeries with loads of awful cacti.'

'Actually, some cacti can be quite stunning when they flower.' Kellah latched onto Teri's misapprehension with wild relief. 'Um, did you need me for something?' she asked, steering the conversation away from flowers in general.

'Oh, yes.' Teri made a small face. 'David Dukes just called. Apparently he's had a rotten weekend. Ethan's ears are playing up again. He wondered if you'd see him early so he can get to work.'

'Yes, of course.' Kellah felt immediate sympathy for the sole supporting father. It was obvious they would have to do something further about his four-year-old son's recurring ear infections. She'd have to refer him. 'Can he come straight in?'

'Yep. He said they were ready to roll, if you could fit him in.'

Kellah glanced at her watch. The family lived barely a block away. They could be at the surgery in a few minutes. 'Call David back then and confirm, please, Teri. Oh, by the way who's in and who's out?'

'Tony's just in and the Hunk's doing hospital visits.' Teri grinned irrepressibly. 'Want me to fix these up for you?' She deftly scooped up the armful of roses, pouting prettily. 'Could I possibly pinch a couple for Reception, do you think?'

But they're mine! Kellah's immediate reaction was to protest. *Jude meant them for me.* Instead, she managed a passably nonchalant smile. 'Help yourself.'

'Terrific. Thanks so-o much,' Teri lilted. 'I'll do my best arrangement and whip them back to you.'

Kellah sank into her chair, her drummed-up smile fading, chased away by a burning need that made her feel weak at the knees.

'Oh, Jude...' she whispered. 'What are you telling me?'

Closing her eyes and drawing in a deep breath, she forced herself to relax. Her relationship with Jude would sort itself out somehow. Meanwhile, she was a medical practitioner with a job to do. Switching on the computer, she brought Ethan Dukes's file up on the screen.

'I hope you don't think I'm being an over-anxious parent, Kellah.' David Dukes shovelled a hand through his hair, leaving the short strands in disarray.

'David, you know better than that.' Kellah began washing her hands at the basin, having examined the child. 'I've told you before, we don't mess about with ears. This type of infection, left untreated, could result in deafness for your son. And clearly the antibiotics are not providing a solution for him.'

Returning to her desk, her gaze went to the little boy engrossed in the bright Lego on the carpeted floor. Although he was grizzly and obviously in pain, he was momentarily distracted. 'I'm going to refer Ethan to Henry Gwynne. He's an ear, nose and throat specialist.'

David rubbed at the early-morning shadow on his chin. 'And what will he do?'

'He'll do a small operation.' Kellah's gaze was full of compassion and admiration for the young father. He'd told her from the beginning of their doctor-patient association that he and Ethan had been on their own for a long time now, his former wife having baled out and gone back to her career as a model.

'We were probably a bit of a mismatch,' he'd said self-deprecatingly. 'I mean, she was a stunner and I'm...

Well, anyway, we kind of rushed into things. She got pregnant and we married.' He'd huffed a bitter laugh. 'It never worked.'

'So you have custody of Ethan?' Kellah had asked, beginning to compile a history of the Dukes family.

'Absolutely. Well, Shona's not interested.' He'd ground to a halt, his arms tightening around the little boy on his lap. 'We manage pretty well. He's in permanent child-care and my boss is reasonably sympathetic to my situation. But, of course, I can't expect to take days off at the drop of a hat…'

'How are you managing with work and a sick little boy to take care of, David?' With the question, Kellah switched back to the present.

David shrugged. 'Not great. But Mum arrived last night. They've finished shearing so she can give us a few weeks until Ethan's on deck again.' He leaned forward earnestly. 'Now, about this operation, Doc…'

'It's a simple procedure.' Kellah's tone was reassuring. 'As I've explained to you, Ethan's condition means that fluid keeps accumulating in the middle ear. Left untreated, it can thicken like glue and be very painful.'

'So, he could have a real problem, then.'

'Certainly—if we don't act and get him seen by a specialist. Don't look so worried.' She'd seen the panic flare in David's eyes. 'We've caught Ethan in time. And he couldn't be in better hands than Dr Gwynne's. He carries out dozens of these procedures—and he's child-friendly,' she tacked on with a smile.

David nodded, clasping his hands between his knees. 'Will Ethan have to go under?'

'He'll have a general anaesthetic,' Kellah confirmed. 'But everything should be straightforward. The surgeon will make a slit in the eardrum. If there's any gunk hiding there, he'll suck it out and insert a tiny tube called a grommet.'

David frowned. 'Will it be there for the rest of his life?'

'Not at all. More often than not, it drops out naturally after about six weeks when the ear is healthy again.'

'OK…' David took a deep breath. 'Thanks for explaining things. When can we see Dr Gwynne?'

'I'll contact his surgery this morning and stress the urgency for Ethan to be seen. Henry will do the procedure as part of his list at the private hospital. You do have medical insurance, don't you?'

'No worries, Doc.' The young father managed a lopsided grin. 'I'm in the highest medical cover. Well, you have to be, don't you, with kids?'

'It certainly helps if you can afford it.' Kellah swung off her chair and stood to her feet.

'My firm pays half so I've got a good deal all round.' David reached down and swung his son up into his arms. 'You'll let me know when the appointment is? Oh—and do I need a letter from you for the specialist?' he asked.

'Yes, to both your questions, David. You'll be notified about your appointment and I'll do your referral letter shortly and have it delivered to Dr Gwynne's rooms. That'll save you having to come back. Take care, now.' She smiled warmly, standing at the door to see them off.

'We will. And thanks, Doc.' David brushed one finger against his son's cheek. 'Nana'll take the nipper under her wing. We'll be sweet.'

Kellah watched the little family until they'd turned the corner into Reception. Checking her watch, she hesitated for a minute as a dark wing of uncertainty shadowed her thoughts. Something David had said—'We were a bit of a mismatch.'

She gnawed at her bottom lip, recognising a dark spot in the pin-bright happiness she'd felt on finding Jude's roses. 'Is that what *we* are, Jude?' she murmured, crossing her arms and wrapping them around her body as to ward off a chill.

Except for the physical pull between them and the fact that they were both medical practitioners, their life experiences had no parallel. Already, he'd practically lived another lifetime, his experiences a world away from anything she'd known. And he'd been desperately in love. Something Kellah knew she'd never been.

Until now.

She felt her heart skid and flutter, the realisation and the overflow of it washing around her. With a little sigh she closed her office door and went slowly along the corridor to the staff kitchen. She needed a caffeine fix to get her through the rest of the morning.

Jude glanced at his watch as he made his way across the car park to the surgery. He was running late. Kellah was probably knee-deep in patients by now. No time to see her. Damn.

In a reflex action he patted his shirt pocket where his beeper had sat for as long as he could remember. He made a face at his own lapse. What on earth had triggered that? He didn't work in a hospital now. Those days were well and truly behind him.

He pushed through the doors into Reception. 'Morning, Teri.'

'Morning, Jude.' Teri fluttered a hand to her heart. 'Can I get you a coffee?'

'No, thanks. I'd better get on.' He picked up the card for his first appointment. 'Jocelyn Prentice?'

A slender woman in her early forties rose to her feet.

'Come through, please.'

In his consulting room, Jude shoved his case under his desk, washed his hands and took a moment to flick through his patient's file. Then he looked up and smiled. 'What can I do for you today, Mrs Prentice?'

'Please, call me Jo.' The woman sent him a faintly weary smile. 'I'm going dotty with this itch on my arms.'

'OK, let's have a look.' Jude edged his chair closer, his gaze narrowing over the weal-like patches on the woman's skin. 'How long have you had it?'

Jo made a face. 'Weeks, it seems. It goes away and then comes back.'

'What kind of work do you do?'

'I train racehorses. I've tried treating the itchy bits with cold packs. From my work with the thoroughbreds, I know about the principle of cold shrinking the blood vessels and so on.'

Jude raised a dark brow. 'And that didn't help reduce the irritation?'

'For a while. But it's back now with a vengeance. It's affecting my sleep.'

'OK…' Jude swung back to his desk. 'We have a few options here, Jo. Problems like this are sometimes the result of a foreign protein that causes the body to produce histamine.'

'Are you saying it's something I'm eating, Doctor?'

'I wish it were that simple.' Jude steepled his fingers under his chin. 'We only know the causes of itchy skin are many and varied. From food to cosmetics. Detergents to pollens.'

Jo shook her head. 'I come into contact with countless chemicals during my work.'

'Don't we all.' Jude sent her a contained little smile.

'When you go home, make a list of what items you normally buy. That takes in food, toiletries, perfume and so on. Try to work out if you've switched brands now and then.'

'Oh, lord.' Jo made a small face. 'That'll take for ever.'

'Might be worth it, though. But in practical terms there are a couple of things you can do. Avoid extremes of temperature when you have a bath. As near as you can, getting the water to body heat is the best. And scrupulously avoid soap or skin preparations.' Jude pulled his prescription pad towards him. 'In the meantime, I'll give you a script for a cortisone cream.'

'And if things don't improve?'

'I'll refer you to an immunologist. In simple terms, an allergy specialist.' Jude handed over the slip of paper. 'Do you wear long sleeves around the stables?'

'Not always.' Jo looked thoughtful. 'And we've recently had to change our bulk-feed supplier.' She glanced across at Jude with a wry smile. 'I guess I'd better keep my wits about me, hadn't I?'

'Do that.' Jude swung to his feet. 'Be your own detective. If the itch doesn't settle with the use of the cortisone cream, get back to me.'

Jude ploughed on through his patient list. It was later than usual when he broke for lunch. In the staffroom, Maggie told him Tony was at a working lunch with a rep from one of the drug companies and Kellah had been and gone. She was now off making hospital visits. Disappointed, Jude made his own wholemeal sandwich, poured a mug of coffee, muttered something about reading and went back to his consulting room.

'What's up with him?' Sophie lifted a hand languidly, gathering up her hair and letting it fall away.

Teri chuckled. 'Not much from where I'm sitting.'

Maggie looked pointedly over the top of her half-spectacles. 'He's probably catching up on his medical journals.'

Where was he? Kellah fretted. Surely he should have finished for the day by now? For the umpteenth time, she quashed the impulse to go along to his office.

And she had a valid reason to see him, she justified, walking restlessly across to the window—to thank him for the roses. That was if they *were* from him. A sharp sudden ache of longing suffused her and she closed her eyes and murmured, 'Give yourself a break, Kellah. Of course they were from him.'

'Talking to yourself, Doctor?'

'Oh! Jude…' Warmth crawled up her cheeks. He was standing in the doorway, arms folded, a slightly watchful expression in his eyes. He stepped in and closed the door. 'I've been trying to catch up with you all day.'

'Oh, me, too.' Kellah smiled uncertainly. 'Catch you, I mean. The roses were lovely.'

'Oh, good. You liked them.' His gaze was still intent, as if her reaction really mattered to him. 'I didn't want to presume anything.'

She looked at him with a frown. 'Why would you think that?'

'I acted like a clod on Saturday night,' he said, his voice a little gruff. 'I wouldn't have blamed you for shafting me.'

Kellah blinked. That had been the last thing on her mind. The very last thing. For a second the air stopped in her lungs and everything seemed to grind to a halt as his words hung in the air. 'No, Jude—never that…'

He came to her then, gathering her in and twirling her round so that she was backed against the desk.

'Jude! What are you doing?' Her protest ended in a little shriek and he silenced her with a kiss. The weight of his legs anchored her against the desk and one hand cradled the back of her head while the other gently captured her breast with the spread of his fingers.

Kellah murmured her compliance, sliding her fingers into the thickness of his hair, breathing in the masculine essence of him, kissing him back as if her very life depended on his closeness.

'We should end every working day like this.' Something wicked twinkled at the backs of Jude's eyes.

'Should we indeed?' Kellah gave a shaky laugh.

'Definitely.' He drew back, sliding his hands down her arms and linking their fingers. His eyes were locked on hers. 'Good day?' He gave her fingers a little squeeze and let her go.

'Busy. You?'

'Likewise. But I'm not complaining. I'm just glad to have this job. I called into Maternity this morning and saw Tracey. They released her today.'

'I know!' Kellah looked disappointed. 'She'd already left when I did my round. Did you see the bub?'

'Couldn't help myself.' He looked a bit sheepish.

'Did you get to hold her?'

'Nah. It was her bathtime. Oh, Tracey sent her thanks again.'

Kellah's look was wistful. 'We'll probably never see them again.'

'Never's a long time,' Jude dismissed. 'Believe me, I should know.' His mouth compressed and suddenly out of nowhere the atmosphere thickened like a fog rolling in from the sea.

'Jude, everyone has a right to be happy.' Kellah chose her words carefully, as if each one cost dearly.

'Do you think I'm not aware of that?' His voice had risen and tightened.

She swallowed, pressing her hands together against her chest and thought, *If I don't say it now, I never will.* 'You realise you're still combating survivor's guilt, don't you? You have to let go before you can claim the right to grieve,' she insisted desperately.

An ominous beat of silence.

'I don't have to take this from you, Kellah.'

She ignored the closed look on his face. 'You shared your innermost feelings with me, Jude. Did you expect me to react like a block of wood?'

He just looked at her and then turned and walked from the room.

Kellah stood there for several minutes, tear-blinded, thinking, *Go to blazes, Jude Christie.* But she couldn't leave it there, couldn't leave things between them so unfinished.

When she'd dredged up enough control, she marched along to his room and confronted him. 'I don't have to take this from you either, Jude. I'm not into emotional game-playing.'

'Neither am I.' He clamped his bag shut with a gesture of finality. 'So I'll back off.'

'Back off?' Her heart lurched.

'Leave you in peace,' he translated clearly.

'In other words, you're dumping me.'

'No one's dumping anyone.' He met her eyes with a frown. 'Just let's give each other some space for a while.'

She gazed across at him, blinking, not understanding the hard, almost frustrated darkening of his eyes. 'You're running, Jude,' she challenged bitterly. 'I thought you had more guts. Well, stay living in the past. I hope your ghosts make you happy!'

Fighting back sick resentment, she turned and marched stiff-backed from his consulting room.

'Dammit!' Jude picked up the nearest object, which happened to be his diary, and threw it against the wall. 'I don't need this!' His teeth clamped on the muttered words. He certainly didn't need Kellah Beaumont calling him gutless!

With a jagged sigh he threw himself back into his chair, ignoring the tight pain inside his chest. He should have kept his mouth shut about his past. He'd given no thought to Kellah's feelings—just hit her over the head with it. Hell, he was pathetic! Moaning on about a former lover the way he had. Well, he'd lost Kellah now. The hurt in her eyes would haunt him for the rest of his days.

He felt the tightening in his throat. So tight he could barely swallow. He ground out a harsh expletive, scrubbing a hand across his eyes. He couldn't remember when he'd felt so grim and it was all such a mess. But, by heaven, it didn't have to stay that way.

Suddenly full of purpose, he rocked forward and snatched up the phone.

Kellah drove home in a sickening kind of daze. She shouldn't have spoken to him like that. The thought echoed again and again through her head.

He was hurt, desperately hurt, and she'd just walked out and left him. And what she'd said to him—about living with his ghosts. She shuddered, horror and disgust clawing at her throat. How could she have said that?

Her legs moving automatically, stiffly, like a robot's, she got out of her car and walked to her front door. Well, on a personal level she and Jude were finished. But, then, they'd never really got started.

Two out of two, Kellah, she thought bitterly, recalling her failed relationship with Scott. Perhaps you'll be a masochist and try for three one of these days. The hollow laugh stayed locked in her throat as she shoved her key into the lock and opened the door.

Dropping her case on the floor, she went through to the kitchen, her control slipping by the second. At least Jude didn't know she'd fallen in love with him. And now he would never have to know. A lump rose in her throat. She'd just have to pocket what little pride she had left and get on with finding a way to work with him.

Over two weeks on, Kellah was beginning to wonder if they were both deliberately keeping out of each other's way. It hadn't been all that difficult to achieve. Her mouth tightened. Obviously it had helped that Jude had disappeared during the week for a two-day seminar in Sydney.

She glanced at her watch, feeling her insides heave. It was Friday again. He'd arrived for work this morning and they had their weekly staff meeting in less than an hour. Thank heavens Tony would be there to provide some kind of buffer.

'So, Kellah, what are your plans for the weekend?' Tony asked. 'Doing something nice?'

They had finished their staff meeting and were gathering up their paraphernalia.

Kellah's fingers closed on her pen. The effort of trying to keep up the appearance of normality in front of Jude had had her composure sliding every which way. 'I'm driving to Coolum straight after work.' She painted on a bright smile. 'Spending the weekend with my parents.'

Tony grinned. 'I suppose you're having one of those shop-till-you-drop jaunts, hmm?'

'I certainly hope so.' Her voice had a brittle edge and she agonised over whether Jude had noticed it. Well, who cared? She was lying anyway. Shopping was the last thing she intended.

She grimaced inwardly. It was more a case of finding somewhere safe to lick her wounds and be fussed over for forty-eight hours, before she had to return and pretend all over again that everything in her world was peachy perfect.

'How about you, Jude?' Tony was businesslike again. 'Feel OK about covering at the GP centre over the weekend?'

'Absolutely.'

'Good, good,' Tony said a bit too heartily, and gathered up the last of his notes. 'Well, I'm out of here, folks.' He got to his feet, sketching a farewell salute to his colleagues. 'See you both on Monday.'

Desperate not to be left alone with Jude, Kellah scrambled out of her chair.

'Now who's running, I wonder?' Jude's calm appraisal made Kellah's skin warm uncomfortably.

'Look, I know it's belated, but I apologise for that,' she offered stiltedly, feeling her heart begin to thud in slow, suffocatingly heavy strokes.

His shoulder jerked dismissively. 'I reacted like a juvenile. And maybe we needed to yell at each other at that particular moment.'

Except they hadn't. Their exchange, by its measured cutting nature, had resulted in something far more wounding. 'How was the seminar?' she deflected stiffly.

He leaned back in his chair, the navy-blue eyes shuttered so that Kellah was unable to read their expression. 'It was time well spent.'

'Good...' Kellah's tone was brisk through necessity. She looked quickly at her watch. 'I'm all packed so I think I'll hit the road.'

'Drive carefully,' he said gravely. 'There are some lunatics out there. We want you back safe and sound.'

Kellah found she couldn't look at him. She left quietly, and once back in her room she whisked a tissue across her eyes and wished desperately that, instead of driving alone, Jude was going with her to meet her parents.

But that was never going to happen now.

Harbouring those rather bleak thoughts, she hitched up her case, locked her room and made her way out to the car park.

Monday morning.

Hardly able to contain her impatience, Kellah took up a position by the window in her consulting room from where she could see the car park. She was waiting for Jude to arrive and when he did, she was determined to tackle him headon.

Jude's heart flipped when he saw Kellah's car already in its space. Although workwise the weekend had been hellish, she'd been on his mind constantly.

They had to talk. He knew that. He just had to find a time and place. Perhaps even today if the lists were light. He grimaced. Unlikely. They seldom were on a Monday. Just the thought of seeing her put a lightness in his step as he swung out of the car and made his way into the building.

He'd scarcely made it into his office when the door opened and Kellah marched in. 'Welcome back.' His smile was forced. 'Nice weekend?'

She made a dismissive movement with her hand. 'Just where do you get off upsetting my patients, Dr Christie?'

Frowning heavily, Jude moved swiftly from behind his desk, walking past her to close the door. He stood against it and folded his arms. 'I'm sure we don't need the whole practice hearing this. What am I supposed to have done?'

'The Tilley sisters.' To her horror, Kellah felt tears welling at the backs of her eyes. She'd thought of him constantly over the weekend and now for some strange reason she just wanted to throw herself into his arms and for him to hold her as if he'd never let her go. She swallowed. 'Florence and Avril Tilley. Surely you remember?'

'It was a crazy weekend, Kellah. Remind me.'

'Avril has Alzheimer's.'

Jude clicked his fingers. 'OK, I'm with you now. I took the call-out to their home. The younger Miss Tilley—'

'Florence.'

'Florence,' he repeated, 'had taken some prescription tablets by mistake and become dizzy. She'd spilt boiling water on her ankle and foot. I had no option other than to hospitalise her.'

'And you bundled Avril into the respite care centre,' Kellah burst out, her voice reedy with emotion.

Jude's blue gaze scorched her face. 'I didn't *bundle* your patient anywhere, Doctor. I made arrangements for her to be taken care of. And she is being taken care of, isn't she?' he challenged.

'No, she's not!' Kellah swiped a strand of hair back from her cheek. 'I saw her this morning. There were two personal care assistants who are still in their teens bustling her around all over the place and Avril is frightened and weepy.'

Jude made a savage click with his tongue. 'For heaven's sake, Kellah, the lady has Alzheimer's. She's bound to be disorientated away from her normal surroundings. I followed protocol. You weren't here to ask. How did you find out, anyway?' He strode across to the window and turned, facing her.

'Florence asked for a phone and rang me from the hospital early this morning.' Kellah felt most of the anger drain away. 'I'd given her my private number in case she ever needed me after hours.'

Jude raised an eyebrow. 'Was that wise?'

'They're *my* patients,' she insisted, as if that explained everything.

'We've established that,' Jude said with remarkable patience. 'So, in your absence, what should I have done that I didn't do?'

Her throat closed tightly. 'Nothing, I suppose.' She linked her hands together and stood stiffly beside his desk, aware of how unprofessional and infantile her attitude now seemed.

Suddenly, Jude moved. In a few strides he was at her side. 'Let's sit for a minute.' He pulled out a couple of chairs and they sat facing one another. Reaching out, he took her hands, rubbing his thumbs almost absently over her knuckles. 'Now, what can we do to ease things for Avril?'

There was such gentleness in his voice, such entreaty,

Kellah would have been made of ice not to respond. Slowly, she raised her head. 'There's a cousin, Leila McHugh. She and her husband have indicated they'd be available to help out at any time.'

'That sounds promising.'

She nodded. 'I've met them briefly. I'm sure they'd be willing to care for Avril in her own home until Florence is able to manage. All this information is on the Tilleys' file.'

Jude heard the faint censure in her voice and decided to take it on board. 'I wasn't to know that, was I? But, then, knowing how meticulous you are with your patients' history, I should have guessed.'

Kellah bit her lip. 'You were obviously run off your feet.'

He gave a hollow laugh. 'For a while there I thought I was back in A and E. I admit to feeling...stretched. But now you're back I can safely hand over the Tilleys, can't I?'

A tentative smile crept slowly over Kellah's lips. 'I imagine you can. How long will Florence need to be in hospital?'

Jude made a moue. 'A week possibly. I doubt she'll need a skin graft and her circulation seems pretty good. Medically, you've obviously taken great care of her.'

'But not enough to make doubly sure she'd disposed of the old tablets.' Kellah made a small face. 'I should have gone out to Rosewood and collected them from her.'

'In a perfect world you would have. But who of us in a busy practice has that kind of luxury? We do the very best we can.' He gave her hands a reaffirming little squeeze. 'Don't we?'

'I suppose.' Kellah smiled guardedly. 'Sorry I jumped on you.'

'Forgiven.' Jude's mouth compressed slightly. 'I'd never want to hurt you intentionally, Kel...'

'No.' Kellah took a shattered breath. 'I wouldn't want to hurt you either.'

Suddenly the atmosphere between them was electric.

Kellah's body felt as if it were on fire, her heartbeat tripping, gathering speed at a sickening rate. For the longest time they sat there unmoving, each waiting for the other to break the silence.

Finally, she found the strength to slowly withdraw her hands. 'We both have patients waiting, Jude.'

CHAPTER TEN

JUDE wasn't going to make the mistake of rushing Kellah.

The knot of uncertainty tightened in his gut. She was still wary around him—any fool could see that. But midway through the next week, he couldn't wait any longer. After surgery, he knuckled a rap on her door and poked his head in. 'Got a minute?'

Kellah turned from the window where she'd been deep in introspection, told her heart to stay in its rightful place and managed a suitably detached smile. 'Come on in.'

'Are you doing anything on Saturday night?' he asked without preamble.

'I don't know—maybe.' She lifted her shoulders in a little shrug, determined not to be won over so easily.

He looked hesitant. 'Sarah's given me tickets to the final night of the play at the Little Theatre and an invitation to the cast party afterwards.'

'Snap!'

Jude looked faintly startled. 'You have tickets as well?'

Kellah's eyes brimmed with laughter. 'Jilly insisted and instructed me to "ask someone nice".'

Jude's mouth twitched briefly. 'So, have you?'

'Have I what?'

'Asked someone nice?'

Kellah looked wry. 'I left the tickets at the hospital

op shop. They were going to raffle them off and make
a bit of money.'

His blue eyes bored into hers. 'So you can come with
me.'

Kellah's heart began jostling for space inside her
chest. 'I suppose I could.'

'That is, if you think I pass the "someone nice" test.'

'No decision on that yet,' she replied cheekily.

Jude's mouth folded in on a smile. 'Pick you up about
seven-thirty?'

'I'll look forward to it.'

What should she wear?

Kellah sifted through the possibilities, finally deciding
on the dress she'd bought specially for their staff
Christmas party last year. She'd had it dry-cleaned and
it still hung in its protective cover in the wardrobe.

Smiling wryly, she slipped it off the hanger and laid
it across the bed, remembering the day she'd bought it.
Jilly had helped her choose it. They'd had one of those
marathon shopping expeditions and Kellah had been
about to give up and wear something she already owned
when Jilly had twitched back the curtain on the change
room.

'Here, this is you!' She'd thrust the garment at Kellah
with a grin of satisfaction.

Dubiously, Kellah had turned the dress from side to
side. 'It's rather...slinky.'

'So?' Jilly had rolled her eyes theatrically. 'Try it on.
Trust me, Kel. On your figure, it'll look fabulous.'

Which, of course, it had.

Now, as she smoothed the cream silk across her hips,
Kellah knew it was the right choice for this evening with
Jude. After all, it was a kind of first date in public, she

supposed, aware of the faint excitement building inside her as she did a little twirl in front of the mirror.

Jude was right on time. Hastily touching a hand to the back of her hair, Kellah went to let him in.

'Hi…' She blinked out into the soft light, trying not to stare.

He was casually but elegantly dressed in well-cut grey trousers, a darker grey jacket of a distinctive tweed and a soft maroon shirt open at the neck, emphasising his olive-toned skin. One side of his mouth almost smiled and her own mouth curved in response.

'Not too early, am I?' he teased softly.

She shook her head. 'Come in. I'm quite ready.'

'You look lovely.' His gaze darkened as he followed her into the lounge. 'It's a bit nippy outside, though. You may need a jacket or something.'

'I'd already thought of that. I have one somewhere.' She looked around, disconcerted, Jude's presence making her feel vulnerable all over again.

'Is this what you're looking for?' He held up the little cropped jacket, his expression softening as he draped it over her shoulders. 'All set?' He tipped her a lopsided smile and then, tucking her hand through his arm, whisked her outside into the starry night.

The play was wonderful, a light-hearted bit of escapism that left them laughing at the end.

Afterwards, as guests of the cast, they made their way outside to the courtyard where someone had made a rapid transformation of the area since the interval. The space had now taken on a party atmosphere.

Tall satiny-leaved plants dotted the perimeter of the courtyard, the fairy lights strung between them twinkling like myriads of tiny stars. And the round tables had been covered with red-checked cloths with fat lighted candles in the centre of each.

Jude tugged Kellah to his side, tightening his fingers on hers almost fiercely. 'Let's give our respective sisters something to speculate about, shall we?'

So saying, he guided Kellah across to where a bar had been set up. He selected two glasses of red wine and handed one to Kellah. 'Here's to us,' he said deeply, touching his glass to hers. 'And don't look now, but I think the ladies are bearing down on us.'

Kellah almost choked on her mouthful of wine.

With introductions swiftly made, Sarah aimed a mock-punch at her brother's arm. 'You rat, I never thought you'd show. You told me you didn't do plays.'

Jude grinned. 'Changed my mind.'

'I thought you said he was just a colleague,' Jilly whispered in an aside to Kellah.

Kellah merely raised an eyebrow and looked myste-rious. 'The play was excellent, Jilly. Congratulations. And, Sarah.' She turned to Jude's sister with a smile. 'You played a wonderful part.'

'Oh, thanks. It was fun to do.'

'Sarah,' someone called. 'The local press is here. We need you for a photo.'

Sarah flapped a hand backwards in acknowledgment and then placed a quick touch on Jilly's arm. 'You should be in this, too.'

'Oh— OK. Nice to meet you, Jude.' Jilly looked re-luctant to remove herself from the little group. She eyed Kellah, her message clear. 'Be sure to keep a place for us at your table, won't you? This shouldn't take long.'

'Actually, Jillian, we'd planned to just finish our wine and take off.' Jude looked suitably rueful. 'I'm taking Kellah dancing.'

Jilly's mouth fell open. 'In that case, I'll, um, catch you both later. Call me tomorrow,' she muttered to Kellah, before stalking off in her higher than high heels.

'I feel a bit mean, dashing off like that,' Kellah said, as they made their way along the street to Jude's car.

'Tough.' He was unrepentant. 'We're grown-ups, not kids who have to explain themselves. Do you like jazz?' he tacked on casually, as they buckled up and he ignited the motor.

'Mmm, yes, I think so. Some of it anyway. Is that where we're going?'

'I've found a place where they play good all-round stuff.' He turned and gave her a very sweet smile. 'And there's a tiny dance floor as well.'

'Sounds fun.' Kellah laughed, a breathless, slightly strangled little sound. She leaned back against the soft seat leather and let her thoughts anticipate how it would feel to dance with Jude.

And of their bodies moving as one.

Jude drove to the old part of town. 'Business-wise there's not much happening up this way any more.' There was regret in his voice as he pulled his car into a vacant spot along the street.

'Not since they built the shopping mall,' Kellah agreed. 'Pity, I suppose, but that's called progress. So, how did you find out about the jazz club?'

Jude cut the engine and released his seat belt. 'Recent patient. He'd mangled his middle finger doing some plumbing—rather inexpertly, obviously.' He smiled crookedly. 'He told me he was a sax player, concerned he wouldn't be able to front for the group at their usual weekend gig. I asked him where they played and came and checked it out for myself. Here we are.' He pushed open the glass-panelled door and waited for her to go through.

The sultry trumpet sounds of a slow jazz number enveloped them as they made their way down a steep flight of stairs to the cellar-like venue. Heavens! Kellah snapped her head up and drew back. There was intimate and there was *intimate*. This definitely fell into the latter description.

'I know it's a bit cramped.' Jude caught her uncertain look. 'But it's non-smoking and air-conditioned. And they have a wicked dessert menu.'

Kellah laughed, a deep throaty chuckle. 'You didn't come for the jazz at all, did you?'

'Hell, no.' He threw her a simmering look and guided over to a table against the wall. 'I came for the opportunity to hold you close on the dance floor.'

His remark brought the tension slamming back, clogging Kellah's throat and pooling the heat low down in her body. Quite slowly, and without her being aware, Jude's hand closed over her shoulder and he turned her gently towards him.

'I'm not setting you up, Kellah,' he said huskily. 'If anything happens between us, it'll be because we both want it.' He withdrew fractionally. 'Would you like a drink?'

She took a deep breath. 'Don't think so. Coffee might be nice, though.'

'And dessert,' Jude insisted, pressing a kiss on her palm and closing her fingers over it.

'Oh, all right, then.' She gave a reluctant smile, watching him pluck the rather dog-eared menu out of its stand. After a silly light-hearted consultation over the exotic-sounding names, they settled on baked rum bananas and vanilla ice cream.

'I've put on kilos,' Kellah groaned a few minutes later, putting her cutlery down and moving her plate aside. 'How do they make it, do you suppose?'

'It's done on the barbecue,' Jude said knowledgably. 'Bit like a banana split, only fancier. And served warm, of course. Did you enjoy it?'

'It was to die for.' Kellah patted her mouth with her serviette. 'But I'm quitting while I'm ahead.'

'Piker.' He laughed softly. 'Still, it gives us an excuse for a bit of exercise on the dance floor, wouldn't you agree?'

Kellah had no time to think of an answer. Almost before she realised it, she found herself in Jude's arms, where she'd been dreaming about being ever since the subject of dancing had arisen.

With the smokily haunting saxophone solo all around them, she let herself go with the music, resting her cheek against his, allowing him to ease her closer so that their bodies moved as one.

Jude felt his senses heighten almost unbearably. He was nuts about the lady. And he'd thought never to feel that way again. He'd been wrong. So wrong.

As they danced, Kellah could almost feel the tension draining out of him, replaced by something else—something more vibrant and urgent.

She moved her hands from where they were linked around his neck, placing them against his chest, startled to feel the unsteady thud of his heart beneath her palms. A gravelly half-sigh escaped him.

'This feels so good—doesn't it?'

She tipped her head back slightly, meeting the warm caress of his gaze. All at once she felt the slow heat licking at her, drawing her in. 'Yes.'

Jude was watching her, his eyes mirroring what they saw in hers. 'Would you like to leave now?'

She swallowed the tiny seed of uncertainty and nodded.

In seconds they were up the stairs and out in the darkness of the night.

As they walked to where he'd parked his car, Jude wrapped her closely to his side and Kellah slipped her arm around his waist under his jacket, luxuriating in the warmth of his skin through the fine silk of his shirt.

She took a shaky breath when the hard jut of his hipbone clashed intimately against hers, wondering dazedly if this was the night she and Jude would become lovers.

When they pulled into her driveway, Jude cut the engine and snapped off his seat belt. 'Wait for me,' he commanded, and swung out of the car.

At the passenger side of the car, he helped her out, folding his arms around her. In one smooth movement he locked his fingers over the small of her back and eased her up against him. 'Is it all right if I come in?' he asked throatily.

Kellah's nerves were jangling. She knew he was asking far more than that. But she couldn't send him away—not when her body was crying out for him. She nuzzled a kiss to the little hollow in his throat 'I guess we can't stand out here in the street indefinitely.'

'No.' A soft laugh rose in his chest. 'Might look a bit odd by the morning.'

The morning. Kellah suppressed another avalanche of nerves. Reaching up, she wound her arms around his neck. 'A kiss might be helpful, though, before we go in.'

'My pleasure...'

Eventually, they stopped kissing and walked up the path arm in arm.

'Oh, not again!' Kellah felt the bunch of keys slide from her hand as she went to open the door.

Jude bent down to fossick for them. 'Are you trying to tell me something?' he asked dryly. Straightening, he shoved the key in the lock and pushed the door open.

'That I'm hopeless with keys?' Kellah gave a strangled laugh and went in front of him into the lounge room. Throwing her clutch bag onto the coffee-table, she turned to him, crossing her arms and kneading her fingers against her chest. 'Um, it's still early. Could we dance some more?'

A beat of silence.

'Kellah…' Jude's voice was rich with gentle humour as he hugged her. 'This isn't some kind of trial we have to go through here. I don't see any judges in white wigs about the place, do you?'

'No…' Embarrassed he'd seen right through her gauche little statement, she buried her face against his chest.

'We're in this together,' he murmured huskily, stroking the back of her hair. 'We'll take it slow and if it means we dance all night then so be it.'

She laughed shakily. 'I don't think it will come to that. Do you…?'

Slowly, Jude pulled back, and they waited there a moment, staring into each other's eyes, and then he took her wrist and raised it to his mouth. 'I wouldn't have thought so.'

His heart did a somersault in his chest. *She's so beautiful*, he thought, taking in the dark sweep of her eyelashes against the fairness of her skin. Her hair still intrigued him, loose and tousled, silky soft. He took a deep breath. 'Uh, what kind of music do you have?'

They found something slow and smooth and Kellah

decided to throw all her uncertainties to the winds, an almost lazy sensuality permeating her body.

Jude put his hands around her waist and she slid her arms around his neck and raised her face for his kiss, her whole body seeming to melt when their lips met. His hands stroked her back, encircled her hips, burning through the fabric of her dress as if his fingers were on fire.

Still kissing, swaying together almost imperceptibly to the music, they made it very slowly up the stairs to the bedroom. Outside the door, they drew back and Jude cupped her face in his hands and stared deeply into her eyes. He nodded infinitesimally, as though he'd seen what he'd wanted to see.

As she pushed the door open and they stepped inside, Kellah faltered, her eyes taking in the softly lit space, one bedside lamp giving out a gentle glow across the pillow. She was inexplicably overcome with nerves. This was such a gigantic step. She bit down on her bottom lip.

'Kellah? If this isn't what you want...'

'No.' She shook back her dark tangle of hair. 'I mean yes. It is what I want. *You're* what I want, Jude.'

'Oh, God, you have me.' His fragile control shattered and he wrapped her in his arms.

Kellah gasped, feeling his matching urgency as he slid down the zip on her dress, letting it pool around her ankles.

'You're beautiful,' he whispered, bending to put his mouth to the hollow between her breasts. 'I knew you would be.' Straightening, he shrugged off his jacket and tossed it aside.

'Let me now.' Kellah tried to undo the buttons on his shirt but he had to help her, and when the last two defeated them both he dragged the shirt over his head in his haste to be rid of it.

Jude shucked off the rest of his clothes and in seconds he was drawing her down with him onto the bed. She shivered, wrapping her bare legs around his, feeling the roughened scatter of hair on his chest as he gathered her in.

They were made for each other. Kellah gave herself as she never had. And Jude was the lover she'd always dreamed of, taking her on a voyage of the senses where longing and need became loving and giving, their journey to fulfilment like a wild dance that left them both shaken with emotion.

For a long time afterwards they just held each other. Eventually, Jude turned on his side so that they faced each other. 'Beautiful girl,' he murmured, lifting a hand lazily and combing his fingers back through her hair.

With a little sigh, she closed her eyes and burrowed in against him.

Kellah realised she must have fallen asleep because she woke with a start to find the bed empty. Her heart wrenched. Surely he hadn't run out on her—not after everything they'd been to each other. Throwing back the covers, she slid out of bed, groping for her robe on the back of the door and dragging it on.

Her bare feet made no sound as she padded down the stairs. On the bottom step she paused and looked through to the lounge room. What she saw sent a shiver right through her.

Jude was there. He was sitting on the sofa, his head bowed as if he was staring at the floor—or at something he was holding.

As she moved up behind him, she could see that, except for his trousers, he was still undressed. Was that a good omen or not? she agonised.

'Jude.' She placed a hand on his bare shoulder.

His head jerked up and he turned, an almost feverish look in his eyes. 'Kellah…' He snapped his wallet shut and stuffed it into his back pocket.

But not before Kellah had seen what he'd been looking at.

It was a snapshot. Even in the diffused light from the table lamp, she could see it was a close-up of a woman's face, her head tossed back in laughter. Angela.

'Uh, I didn't hear you come in.' His face worked for a second. 'What's up?'

What was he—some kind of a joker? Kellah pulled her hand away from his shoulder as if she'd been stung. 'You're still living with your ghosts, I see,' she said bitterly. 'I won't let you go on doing this to me, Jude.'

There was a moment of stunned silence before he uncoiled to his feet. 'Kellah, wait a minute. I can explain.'

'Don't even try.' She backed away, closing her eyes briefly and then forcing herself to look at him. 'Because I don't want to listen—not any more.'

He put his hands out and gripped her shoulders. 'Kellah, it's not what you think.'

'Get your hands off me!' Her voice came out cracked and she swallowed thickly. 'Just—just—get the rest of your clothes and get out of here.'

Turning, she bolted into the kitchen, only daring to move when she heard the throb of his car engine fade away.

Kellah felt frozen. A glance at the kitchen clock told her it was still the early hours of the morning. She didn't

know what to do. Too drained to think, she reached into
the top cupboard and withdrew a bottle of whisky. Then
taking a glass, she poured herself a small measure. She
had to get warm.

She sat on a kitchen stool, taking sips of her whisky,
feeling the liquor gradually begin to warm her insides.

She couldn't go back to bed—not with the scent of
Jude everywhere. She hugged her arms across her
breasts. Even after what he'd done, she still craved his
touch, still ached for his body inside hers.

Yet he'd gone without a word. But you told him to
go, the rational part of her brain insisted. *You told him
to go.*

'Oh, lord,' she whispered through a choked throat.
'Was I too hard on him? And where is he now?'

Jude didn't go home. Instead, he drove to an all-night
diner on the outskirts of town. He ordered a pot of coffee
and sat in a corner booth and promised himself he'd
make Kellah listen even if it killed him—or if *she* killed
him.

Kellah finally slept fitfully on the downstairs sofa. It was
still barely six o'clock when she woke fuzzily, no nearer
an understanding of what she wanted or needed. It
seemed an awful effort to shower and dress but she felt
marginally better after pulling on jeans and a navy long-
sleeved sweatshirt and running a comb through her hair.

It was a long time before she registered the ringing of
the doorbell. Her heart lurching sickeningly, she went to
answer it.

'Oh, Jude…' Her hand went to her throat. 'I thought
it might have been the police.'

'Why the police?' He frowned heavily. 'What've you done?'

'Nothing.' She shook her head. 'I thought you might have had an accident and they'd come to tell me...'

His frown deepened. 'You're not listed as my next of kin. Why would they come here?' He sighed. 'And why are we having this ridiculous conversation on the doorstep?'

Letting her breath go on a shaky sigh, she said, 'You'd better come in.' She made an awkward little gesture with her hand and turned back into the room. The front door closed quietly behind Jude, and he followed her through to the kitchen. 'I've just made tea. Would you like a cup?'

'Sounds good.' He moved closer to her.

Very aware of him beside her, Kellah got down one of her blue and white striped mugs. She bit gently at her bottom lip. He seemed ill at ease and there was an air of vulnerability about him. She poured the tea and handed the mug to him, forcing herself to meet his eyes. Her heart turned to marshmallow. 'Would you like something to eat?'

'No, this is fine.' He took the mug a bit awkwardly. 'Can we talk?' He looked around for another kitchen stool.

They sat side by side at the counter, their knees almost touching. And for a few awful seconds there was silence.

Kellah's heart was pounding, uncertainty spreading to every part of her body.

'Uh, it's probably best if I say what I have to say.' Jude frowned down at his tea-mug and then his gaze lifted to hers. 'And then you can decide if you want anything more to do with me.'

Her eyes wide, frightened almost, she whispered, 'All right.'

'I haven't behaved very fairly of late, have I?' He stopped for a moment and pressed a hand across his eyes. 'I knew I had unresolved issues from my time in Afghanistan and you were right to say I needed further counselling. I've done that.'

'You have?' Faintly bewildered, she sank her elbow on to the bench and rested her chin in her hand. 'When?'

'Last week. I wasn't at any seminar, Kel. I had two days of intensive counselling with a grief therapist. I managed to get a referral to a brilliant chap who'd been all through the conflict in East Timor as an MO attached to the armed forces. He knew exactly where I was coming from. I managed to get it all out. And afterwards...' he blinked for a moment '...I felt like a ton weight had been lifted from me.'

Kellah nodded blankly. She was glad for him—so thankful he'd found some kind of peace with his past. But... She moistened her lips. 'So what was last night all about, then?'

'The photo.' Watching her, his expression guarded, he went on, 'After we'd made love, I couldn't sleep. I was wound up—drenched with emotion. So I got up. When I pulled my trousers on, my wallet fell out. I still had it in my hand when I went downstairs. I flicked it open—not for any specific reason—and I found the picture of Kamal I've always carried. I pulled it out and the one of Angela was behind it. I hadn't even remembered it was there.'

Her mind a whirlpool of jumbled thoughts and emotions, Kellah said starkly, 'Were you comparing what you'd had with her and—us?'

'Hell, no! Nothing like that!' His voice tightened and

there was a long pause. 'I finally realised I could let her go…'

'Oh…' Kellah's voice was a thread. 'Oh, Jude…' She put her hands to her cheeks and felt the dampness there. 'I feel so guilty now.'

He made a rough sound in his throat. 'That's the last thing you should feel. You've hung in there, waded through all my baggage where most women would've run a mile.'

'I was tempted.' Her laugh was fractured, sheer relief running through her like sweet, clear rain. 'But something made me stay. And here we are.' Leaning forward, she took his face between her hands and gently lowered it to meet her mouth.

'Kel…' Jude's kiss was hungry yet achingly sweet and like two rivers flowing together, they slowly slid off their high stools and went into each other's arms.

After the longest time they drew apart.

Jude's mouth twitched ruefully. 'I'd kill for a shower.'

'Go ahead.' Kellah lifted a hand and touched his cheek. 'And while you're doing that, I'll make breakfast.'

They were eating outside in the courtyard again. The sun was already strong, delineating the shadows of the potted shrubs like wavy, dark cut-outs across the paved surface.

Kellah sliced a section off her fried egg and married it with a corner of bacon. She smiled reminiscently. 'I used to call this crispy part of the egg-white the lace when I was a kid.'

'Cute.' Jude sent her an indulgent look.

Lover-like, she leant over and pecked him on the cheek. 'So, what are you doing for the rest of the day?'

'I promised to look in on the Muirs at home.' Jude

took another piece of toast from the rack. 'As you know, I'm monitoring Tally for this trial being conducted by the Jarvis Institute. And Lauren's anxious to show off Tally's progress with this new breathing technique.'

'Her asthma's improving, then?'

'In leaps and bounds. The physio's got her doing some water aerobics as well.'

'It's lovely when a patient takes off, isn't it?' Kellah knew exactly where he was coming from.

'It's not all down to me,' he insisted. 'We collaborated, if I remember. Your insights were invaluable.'

She looked up at him from under her lashes and smiled. 'In other words, I'm a clever clogs.'

'Yep.' Jude scooted his chair back. 'Coffee?'

'Mmm. Thanks.'

Jude paused, his fingers spread over the back of his chair. 'My spirits feel so light I could take off and fly over the treetops.'

'Mine, too.' Kellah's teeth caught the bottom edge of her lip as she grinned.

Much later, they said a lingering farewell.

'What are you going to do now?' Jude sent her a questioning, crooked smile.

Kellah rolled her eyes heavenward. 'Pour myself a stiff drink and call Jilly, I suppose.'

Jude pretended to shudder. 'I'll probably have Sarah's inquisition on my answering-machine when I get home.'

'Should we say something—or nothing?' Kellah wondered aloud.

'Just telling them to mind their own business might be more to the point,' Jude growled.

'We can't do that!' Kellah gave him a little admonishing shake. 'They mean well.'

'Yeah.' He cracked a hard laugh. 'So does the dentist when he shoves the drill in your mouth.'

Somewhat to his surprise, Jude found no message from Sarah when he got home. But next day she arrived at his office just after his morning surgery.

'Hi, big brother.' She popped her head around the door. 'Teri said you'd finished.'

Without looking up from the notes he was writing, Jude beckoned her in. After a minute he tossed his pen aside and gave her his full attention. 'How're things, Sari?'

'Fine, thanks.' Her mouth twitched. 'You haven't called me that in ages. You must be feeling pleased with life.'

'Not bad.'

'Did you and Kellah enjoy yourselves on Saturday night?' she asked sweetly.

'Yes, thank you.'

Sarah looked marginally more confident. 'You looked good together, Jude.'

'Because we're both tall?'

'Very droll.' Picking up a paper clip from his desk tray, she flicked it across at him. 'Jilly thought so, too.'

'Good. I'm glad we've dealt with that.'

'You're a meany, Jude.' Sarah howled her frustration. 'You know I only want to see you happy again.'

'I know you do...' Jude's gaze softened. He chewed his lip for a second. 'Kellah's a very special lady. That's all there is to tell at the moment.'

'But that's fabulous!' Sarah sighed dramatically. 'Isn't it fabulous, Jude?'

He lifted one shoulder in a shrug. 'Perhaps it'll be too *fabulous* to last. I don't want to pre-empt anything and

I want your solemn word this goes no further, Sarah. Deal?'

'Oh, for heaven's sake! I run a newspaper. I do have some sense of confidentiality. Oh, by the way.' She dug into her carry-bag. 'This came for you this morning.'

Jude's gaze narrowed on the envelope with its distinctive logo in the corner. 'Why are they writing to me now? And why to your address?'

'Probably because it was the one you gave them when you started wandering around the world,' Sarah said pointedly. 'Aren't you going to open it?'

'Later.' Indifferently, he tossed the envelope aside.

'Now, if you don't need me for anything else, I have a house call to make.'

'Oh. Yes, I do, actually. Hang on.' Sarah delved into her bag again. 'I have a couple of medical queries for the column, if you wouldn't mind helping me out.'

'When do you want them?' Jude lifted his arms behind his head and stretched.

'Soon as you can.' She tipped him an impish grin as she got to her feet. 'If you can spare the time away from your love life, of course.'

Jude unwound, as if to chase her, and then sank back in his chair. A wry smile flickered around his mouth. 'When's Joe back?' he asked instead.

'Couple of weeks.' Sarah's smile faded. 'I never thought when I married a bank officer he'd end up jetting all over the world.'

'He's good at what he does,' Jude said practically. 'That's why. And think of the money he makes.'

'Mmm. There is that,' she conceded. 'But this time I hope he's home for good. Isaac and I miss him to bits.' She turned at the door and waggled her fingers. 'Byee. Give Kellah my best.'

Jude was still chuckling when Kellah knocked and came in. He swung to his feet and gathered her in, gripped by a blinding pleasure at just seeing her. 'Good morning,' he said softly, and kissed her lingeringly. 'Or is it afternoon?'

'A bit of both, I think.' Kellah tucked herself in against him. 'Was that Sarah I just saw leaving?'

'Mmm. She left some mail for me.'

'Oh. Sorry.' She looked down at the envelope on his desk and flashed him a questioning look. 'Am I inter-rupting? Did you want to get to it now?'

'No.' He touched his mouth to hers. 'I'll open it later.'

'Oh, OK. Are you free for lunch? I've brought sand-wiches and we could grab a take-away coffee and sit in the park.'

'I would have loved to.' Jude's mouth pleated at the corners in a moue of disappointment. 'But I've a house call to make. Old Alby Nissel. A neighbour rang. Apparently, he's very poorly. Too weak to come to the surgery.'

'Poor old chap.' Kellah frowned. 'Alby's been one of Leo's patients for ages. He may need to be hospitalised.'

'Possibly.' Jude looped his fingers over her shoulders and squeezed. 'I'll know more when I've seen him. Meanwhile, rain-check on lunch in the park?'

She nodded, recognising the little spiral in her tummy as pure unadulterated happiness.

'Have you talked to Jilly?' Jude spun away to collect his bag.

'Briefly.' Kellah made a small face. 'They were on their way out when I rang. She's going to return my call tonight. I want to tell her about us, Jude. Do you mind?' She watched the tiny pulse flicker in his cheek and added hastily, 'Not *everything*, of course. Just that, well, that we're seeing each other…'

'That's fine with me.' He opened his medical case and checked the contents. Snapping the locks shut, he brought his head up, his mouth compressing on a very sheepish smile. 'Actually, I've spilt the beans to Sarah,' he confessed. 'Not in Technicolor but enough to keep her happy—do *you* mind?'

'You old softie.' Kellah shook her head. 'Yesterday you were all for telling everyone to mind their own business.'

He lifted one shoulder in a shrug. 'Well, as you pointed out, they mean well. And Sarah's always been there for me so I figure I owe her a measure of honesty. Besides, it'll get her off my back for a while,' he ended, on a half-laugh. He paused with his hand on the door. 'Just a thought—now we're not able to do lunch, would you feel like keeping me company on the drive out to Alby's place?'

Kellah felt her heart zing. With both of them having such busy schedules, she'd been wondering just when they were going to find time for each other. 'I'd love to. But I'd better let Maggie know in case there's an emergency of some kind.'

Five minutes later, they were in Jude's car and heading for the rural reaches of the town to an area called One Tree Hill. Kellah had brought her sandwiches and they were tucking in as they drove.

'Any idea what Alby's line of work was before he retired?' Jude asked.

'He was a miner. But that was in the days when it was all underground. More recently the deposits of coal have moved much nearer the surface, so open-cut mining is mostly the go, which must be a blessed relief for the families.'

'To say nothing of the workers themselves,' Jude grunted. He spun her a quick look. 'Maggie drew me a bit of a mud-map of the road to Alby's. It's in the glove box. Mind getting it out and being my navigator?'

'No need.' She let her hand rest briefly on his thigh. 'I did a house call for Leo out here not so long ago. Alby still lives in one of the miners' cottages. I can direct you straight there.'

Alby's cottage looked even more dilapidated than when she'd been here recently, Kellah thought sadly. Alby was an old man now. Surely after his years of hard work he deserved to be housed better than this.

She shook her head. It wasn't fair he had to live in this old shell of a place—untended, paint peeling, the broken-down front fence held up by decades-old grape-vines. Which might be all right when they were produc-ing, but at the moment they were awfully depressing, their autumn-bare branches like so much rotten old scaf-folding.

The metal gate squeaked loudly on its hinges as Jude opened it, and Kellah half-expected Alby to come tot-tering to the front door to greet them. But according to the neighbour, the old fellow was too ill to be doing much at all.

'OK, let's see what we've got.' Jude opened the sag-ging front door and they went in. 'Mr Nissel!' he called. 'It's the doctor.'

There was no answer.

'Would the neighbour have taken him to her place?' Kellah wondered aloud.

'That wasn't the message Maggie got.' Jude began striding up the short hallway. Something was wrong here. He could feel it. He called again, 'Alby, are you there?'

'Oh, Jude, look…' Kellah gave a gasp as they entered the small lounge room. Alby looked as though he'd been anchored in the shabby armchair for ever. 'Has he had a stroke, do you think?'

'Don't know.' Jude dropped his bag and bent over the elderly man. 'Alby, it's Dr Christie. Can you hear me?'

Alby's eyes fluttered open and then closed.

'I'll call an ambulance.' Kellah slid her mobile from her blazer pocket.

'We need priority on this,' Jude snapped. 'He's dangerously dehydrated. I'd say he hasn't eaten anything substantial for days. And where the hell is this so-called neighbour?'

'Ambulance is on its way.' Kellah pocketed her mobile. 'How is he?' she asked, watching as Jude ran his stethoscope over Alby's chest and back.

'A few rattles.' Jude's mouth tightened. 'Possibly fluid.'

Kellah put her hand to the old man's forehead. 'He's feverish, Jude.'

'I know. He's very ill. I'll get a drip in. And grab that blanket off the sofa there, please, Kellah.'

'Give me a hand.' Kellah unfurled the blanket and Jude helped her tuck it around their patient. She bit her lips together. Were they going to lose this special old man? 'I'll hunt up some night things for him to take to the hospital.'

'OK. I'll try to make him more comfortable.' Jude snapped open his case. 'Got everything?' He looked up as Kellah returned with a small overnight bag. 'You're as white as a ghost.' He frowned heavily. 'Is everything all right?'

'No, it's not.' Kellah said with an effort. 'Alby's bed-room is in chaos. I think someone's tried to rob him.'

Jude swore under his breath. 'What kind of scumbags would rob a sick old man, for crying out loud?'

'They've slit the mattress open.'

'Probably looking for money.' Jude's frown deepened. Kellah sank shakily on to the edge of a chair. 'Can we assume it was one of the thieves who called the sur-gery, then?'

'How would they know what doctor he went to?' Jude had his head bent, monitoring Alby's pulse.

'There was an appointment card from the surgery next to the bedside lamp. They could've seen that and taken a chance.'

'But not before they'd trashed the place. Bastards...' He tucked Alby's hand back under the blanket. 'Don't touch anything else, Kellah.' He snapped his mobile out of his back pocket. 'I'm calling the police.' He stabbed out the emergency number.

Kellah felt a cold river of dread run down her spine. 'You don't think they're still around, do you?'

Jude's face grew grim. 'You can bet your boots they've scarpered but if they've left fingerprints, it might give the police a lead.' His head came up, listening. 'That sounds like the ambulance now. Hello, police?' He turned away, speaking into his mobile as his call was answered.

'Mr Nissel is exhibiting early signs of pneumonia,' Jude briefed the paramedics a little later. 'Slight audible wheeze plus crackles on bases of both lungs. The ad-mitting reg should X-ray immediately on arrival.'

'Right you are, Doc.' The officers wheeled the stretcher into place. Very gently, they lifted Alby. 'Come on, matey. It's hospital for you, old-timer. Easy does it now.'

'Should we wait for the police?' Kellah asked, when the ambulance had driven away and they'd walked back inside.

Jude glanced at his watch. 'If we do, it's going to make us late for afternoon surgery. There's nothing more we can tell them anyway. They'll find exactly what we found. And if they need us for anything, they'll know where to find us.'

They gave a cursory look around, then made their way along the hallway, pulling the front door closed as they left.

'I'll get onto the housing commission without delay and see what they've got available,' Kellah said firmly, standing beside Jude as he returned his medical case to the boot of his car. 'Alby can't come back here.'

'Hmm.' Deep lines grooved the edges of Jude's blue eyes as the beginning of a frown appeared. 'Alby may not make it, Kel,' he said quietly.

Kellah looked stricken. 'Is there something you're not telling me, Jude?'

'No. But you saw how ill he was. On the other hand, let's think positively. If you feel you want to enquire into his housing, do it by all means. Who owns the cottage, do you know?'

'The mining company,' she said flatly. 'They own dozens. They're all under some kind of perpetual lease, I think.'

'Then it's time they did something about maintaining them.' Jude's tone was scathing. 'If you're determined about this, I'll back you up. We'll put a rocket under these fat cats. We'll get onto the local MP as well. Time they all did something to earn their salaries.'

'Thank you!' Kellah was deeply touched. In a spontaneous action she reached up and wound her arms around his neck.

His arms encircled her. 'For what?'

'Supporting me. Going to bat for Alby.'

'Helping you kick butt, you mean.' Laughing softly, he whirled her in a circle, then gathered her in, his eyes on her face with the intensity of a camera lens. For the longest moment the world seemed to turn on its axis and then: 'Marry me, Kellah.'

CHAPTER ELEVEN

KELLAH'S mouth dried.

He'd taken her breath clean away. Marriage. She savoured the word in her head and then hesitantly on her tongue. *'Marriage?'*

'Mmm.' Jude smiled at her bewildered expression. 'Nice, old-fashioned word, isn't it? It means intimate union,' he murmured, his mouth at her ear.

A shiver went through her. 'But it's such an enormous decision,' she protested weakly. 'Do you—'

'Know how I feel about you?' he said deeply. 'I love you, Kel. It's as simple and as complicated as that.' He kissed her, a tender, hungry, loving kiss. 'Do you need time to think about it?'

'Yes—I mean no, I don't have to think about it. Oh, yes, Jude! I'll marry you.' Tears came from nowhere and blocked her vision. 'It's like a dream...'

'We're wide awake, Doc.' He kissed her tears away. 'We're getting married.'

'Yes...' She laughed her delight. 'I can't wait.'

They both groaned in frustration when his mobile rang.

'Later.' He captured her hand and pressed his mouth to her wrist.

'That was Maggie.' Jude's expression was tight, as he closed his phone. 'There's been an accident at the old colliery. She said you'd know where it was.'

'It's only about a kilometre from here.' She flapped an encompassing hand. 'One Tree Hill was all under

163

mining once. What's happened?' she demanded, as they
flew back into the car and Jude started the engine. 'The
mining stopped here years ago.'

'Apparently, it's a demolition job—one of the old
buildings that was to be taken to a heritage site. It's
collapsed. Two workers, serious injuries.'

Kellah frowned. 'Couldn't the hospital have sent
someone from A and E?'

'There's a major road trauma somewhere.' Jude
gunned the car along the narrow bitumen road. They did
a ring around the GPs and as we were already halfway
there, we got the gig. But at least they can spare us an
ambulance. It's on its way.'

Kellah crossed her hands, rubbing at her upper arms
as if she were cold. She hated this. The uncertainty. Not
knowing what was at the end of an emergency call-out.
She'd never had the stomach for the accident and emergency department. It was one of the reasons she'd gone
into private practice. 'Is Maggie going to juggle our afternoon lists?'

Jude's mouth drew in. 'As best she can. It's lightish
anyway and Tony can take anything urgent. I'm just glad
I made the decision to always carry an extra trauma pack
with me wherever I go.'

Kellah sent him a guarded look. 'Perhaps that stems
from your time in Qandahar.'

He shrugged. 'Maybe. I just know, as a medical practitioner, it makes me feel less vulnerable somehow.'

'We're almost there.' Kellah's words seem to echo in
the close confines of the car. 'There'll be a sign at the
turning on the left.'

'Did they ever have a mining accident here?' Jude
took the turning at speed.

'Yes.' Kellah felt the nerves in her stomach react, her

gaze taking in the desolate sight of bony ridges and windblown tussocks as they got closer to the site.

'Bad one?' Jude persisted.

She made a choked sound. 'They're all bad, Jude. But I remember this one particularly. It was the one in which Dane Muir lost his life. It happened just as the night shift of twenty men had begun work. A sudden explosion of methane gas and coal dust erupted in one of the tunnels. Nine miners managed to escape. But it was considered too dangerous to attempt to rescue the remaining eleven. A second explosion the next day put paid to any hope of the men remaining alive. The mine was sealed off and closed.'

'Sweet God.' Jude shook his head. 'Makes going to work as a GP almost a doddle in comparison, doesn't it? Ah, this looks like us.' He slowed the Audi and pulled to a stop beside a set of ramshackle buildings.

A man at the site moved quickly to meet them. 'Are you the doctors?'

Jude stuck out his hand. 'Jude Christie and this is Kellah Beaumont.'

'Jim Matthews. I'm the foreman.'

Jude strode to the boot of his car. 'What's the damage, Jim?'

'Two of my best lads.' The foreman was almost wringing his hands. 'They were up high, getting the roof off. The whole thing collapsed, shot them through into the bowels of the building. One's been caught under a bloody great beam. The other lad is out to it. He bounced off scaffolding as he fell.'

'How far did they fall?' Kellah snapped the question, taking Jude's medical case while he hitched up the trauma pack.

'About twenty feet, I reckon.'

So there could be multiple injuries. Kellah bit her lips tightly together as they ran to the accident scene. Oh, lord. She jerked to a stop and looked frantically at the foreman. 'Is it safe to go in?'

'I reckon. All that can fall has already fallen down.'

Jude's expression became grim. 'Can we have their names, please?'

'Sure, Doc. Perry Barwick and Shane Phelan.'

Kellah gave a gasp of horror. 'Shane has a brand-new baby!'

'Yeah, I know.' Jim's voice broke. 'He took some leave. This is his first day back.'

'Which man is unconscious?' Jude shot the question hardily.

'Perry.'

'Right, we'll see to him first.'

Perry Barwick's face looked glassily pale against his navy-blue work shirt. Jude squatted beside him. 'Get a BP reading, Kel.' He put his hand to the injured man's wrist and shook his head. 'Barely there.' He whipped a torch out of the trauma pack. 'Dammit,' he swore softly, 'his pupils are all over the place.' He shot a look at Kellah, his gaze widening in query.

She shook her head. 'Seventy over forty.' There was no question the young man was in serious trouble. Very possibly he was bleeding internally. Kellah held the elasticised waistband of Perry's shorts away from his body so Jude could palpate his stomach.

'Hard as a rock.' His breath hissed out sharply. 'Get a line in, Kellah. There'll be a flask of blood product in the trauma kit. We'll run it as fast as we dare and hope that holds him until we can get him to surgery.'

'Here's the ambulance now,' Kellah said with relief.

'Right.' Jude grabbed his bag. 'I'll look at Shane.'

'This one for us, Doc?' One of the paramedics hunkered down beside Kellah.

'Please.' Kellah gave their findings quickly, adding, 'Suspected ruptured spleen. Would you alert Resus, please? He'll need to go straight to surgery.'

'Shane?' Jude squatted close to where the young worker lay pinned under the beam. 'It's Jude Christie. We'll have you out of here soon, mate. Can you hang on?'

'Sure Doc…' Shane's voice was thin with strain. 'Can you let Tracey know I'm OK?'

That was presuming he was. Jude's lean, rugged face was stretched tautly. 'Jim tells me he's already done that. And there's a crane on the way, buddy. They'll have that log lifted off you in no time flat.'

'I think me leg's history, Doc.'

'Well, as far I know, we can still fix legs. Might have a bit of hardware inside you but as long as you don't go near any lightning strikes, you should be OK.' Jude turned sharply as Kellah dropped beside him. 'Where the hell is that second ambulance?'

'There isn't one to spare. The same one will have to come back for Shane. How is he?' she asked quietly.

Jude gave a noncommittal grunt. 'We'll know more when we get this blasted log off him. Certain fracture if I'm any judge. I'm going to crawl in somehow and give him a shot of morphine.'

Kellah caught his hand. 'Mind how you go. It looks like a bomb site.'

'Jim assures me it's stable. It's just a matter of watching where I put my feet.'

Almost two hours later the beam had been lifted and they were free to work on Shane.

'God know what his circulation's doing,' Jude said grimly.

Kellah drew the space blanket carefully to one side. Poor young guy. She held back her own distress. Shane had a *complete* fracture if ever she'd seen one.

'Am I goanna lose me leg, Doc?' His voice was a trace of sound.

Kellah opened her mouth and closed it, meeting Jude's eyes for an intense second before each looked away.

'Stick with it, Shane.' Jude avoided answering the injured man's question. 'We're going to splint your injured leg to your good one now. That'll mean less trauma for you when the guys lift you on to the stretcher. You'll be in hospital soon.'

What a day. Kellah watched as the ambulance left the scene, bouncing and gliding over the rough terrain. Stifling a sigh, she began repacking the trauma kit, securing the sharps they'd used for safe disposal later.

Turning her head, she looked to where Jude was in close consultation with Jim Matthews. No doubt there would have to be an accident report put in to the Workplace Health and Safety authority. She just hoped there would no backlash on anyone.

'Sorry I left you with all the clearing-up.' Jude was at her side. 'Here, I'll take that.' He hefted the trauma pack and they made their way back to his car.

In seconds, everything was squared away. 'Let's get out of here.' Jude lifted his arms in a stretch. 'I think a shower and a stiff drink, in that order, are called for, don't you?'

'Sounds good.'

'My place?' He tapped her cheek with a gentle finger. 'We can take a short cut from here.'

Was he asking her to stay the night? Kellah dropped her gaze from his questioning one, focusing instead on the unfastened neck of his pale blue shirt. She swallowed. 'My car's still at the surgery.'

'I'll drop you home early in the morning so you can change for work.'

Kellah looked uncertain. She took a deep breath and expelled it heavily. 'Everyone will know about us, then, won't they?'

Jude's smile was as old as time. 'Do you care?'

'No...' Her answering smile was a bit tentative. 'I guess not.'

It was beginning to feel like home already. Would it be *her* home when they got married? Probably. She doubted Jude would want to move in with her.

There was such a lot they'd have to sort out. Wide-eyed, Kellah stared into the bathroom mirror. At this point everything seemed a bit unreal.

Well, there'd be nothing unreal about it tomorrow when they announced their plans to everyone. Feeling slightly vulnerable, she picked up the towel and began to rub her hair dry. After her shower, she'd dressed again in the trousers she'd worn to work and one of Jude's big warm jumpers.

Ten minutes later she made her way through to the kitchen. And Jude. She pasted a smile on her face. 'Shower's free.'

'Thanks.' He smiled briefly. 'I'll have mine directly.'

Kellah's heart thumped a bit. She supposed they could have had a shower together but neither of them had suggested it. Oh, lord. Were they feeling awkward around one another already? And if so, was that any basis to be thinking they were ready for the intimate life of a married couple?

Jude, oblivious of the tumult inside her, handed her a glass of red wine. 'I guess we should be drinking champagne,' he said wryly. 'We got engaged today. Remember?'

'Yes…' Kellah's fingers tightened around the stem of her glass.

'What's the matter, Kel?' Jude was regarding her steadily. 'Gone off me already?'

'No!' She looked shocked. 'Just a bit…staggered at the speed everything's happened, I suppose.'

Leaning over, he removed the glass and held her hand tightly. 'It feels pretty scary to me, too—to love someone as much as I love you. But whether it's happened quickly or slowly, it's happened. And it feels absolutely right.'

Kellah blinked. He could say that with confidence, she reasoned. He'd been there before—with Angela. 'How do I know what I feel for you will be enough, Jude? Enough to last?'

For a long moment he just looked at her, his gaze never wavering. 'There are no guarantees, Kellah. About anything in life. You've been a doctor long enough to know how people's lives can be altered in a few seconds. I only know at this point my life is so much richer for having found you and fallen in love with you.' He lifted her hand and pressed a kiss to her palm. 'I need you to dream my dreams with me. I'll even take on all the cooking.' His sudden smile was tender and very dear. 'Does that impress you?'

'How could it not?' She laughed, her eyes filling with tears of reaction. She slid her hand up his arm and onto his chest, feeling the heavy beating of his heart under her palm. Her own heart was beating faster, too, racing against her ribs and making it hard to breathe. 'I'm overwhelmed with love for you, Jude.' Her voice was low, husky. 'I've never felt this way before.'

He swallowed convulsively. 'That makes me feel very special...' He tightened his fingers protectively on hers. 'Now, drink your wine and I'll grab a shower. Then we'll do something that will mean far more than any words ever could.'

Making love with him was everything Kellah remembered and more.

She'd been the slightest bit afraid they would be nervous and awkward with each other, panicking that it would all go awry.

She should have thrown her doubts to the winds and conserved her energy. She found she needed every last vestige of it. Jude was tenderly demanding, driving her to heights she hadn't known existed.

Curled together like spoons, they fell asleep.

When the phone rang an hour later, they woke simultaneously. Jude swore colourfully under his breath. 'I forgot to put the answering-machine on.'

'It could be an emergency of some kind.'

'I'm not on call.'

Kellah dug him in the ribs. 'There are other kinds of emergencies, Jude.'

'OK, I'm going.' He hooked on some shorts and disappeared out the door.

He was gone a long time. When he came back, he seemed preoccupied. 'It was Sarah,' he told her without preamble. 'Wanting the stuff for her column.'

'Oh. Did you give it to her?' Kellah pushed herself

into a sitting position and scraped the hair out of her eyes.

Jude snorted a laugh. 'Bit difficult when the readers' letters are still sitting on my desk at the surgery. But it gave me the chance to tell her about us.'

Kellah's heart revved. 'Was she pleased?'

'Already planning the wedding.'

Kellah groaned, bracketing her head in her hands. 'I'd better call Jilly, then, or her nose will be out of joint. What've we started, Jude?' It was a heartfelt wail.

'Fun and games probably.' He dropped onto the edge of the bed beside her. 'Kel, I have something for you…'

'Oh, have you? What is it?' she asked softly, leaning against him and rubbing her cheek against the warmth of his chest.

'Just this.'

'Oh, Jude…' She smiled up at him. 'What a gorgeous little box! It looks centuries old.'

'Not quite. It belonged to my grandmother.'

Kellah's fingers shook as she opened it. Her eyes widened. A ring with the most beautiful setting she'd even seen. The deepest red ruby surrounded by diamonds. 'For me?'

'Of course for you,' he said huskily, as he gently took the ring from its box and slipped it onto the third finger of her left hand. It fitted perfectly. 'You can have it reset if you like.'

'That would be sacrilege! I love it the way it is.' She held it out in front of her. 'It even has a wide band like a modern setting, yet it must be years old.'

'It is.' Jude's look was tender. 'It's been in a strong-box in the bank for yonks. I only recently retrieved it and had it cleaned. Must have known something, mustn't I?' he said against her lips. 'When can we get married?'

'Soon.' Dreamily, Kellah moved her hand so that the ring's precious stones sparkled as they caught the light.

'A month, then?'

'Two.'

'Six weeks,' he bartered.

'Done.'

CHAPTER TWELVE

KELLAH couldn't believe the speed at which arrangements for their wedding began happening.

'Mum and Dad will expect a church do,' Jillian warned, while they were sitting over coffee on the following Saturday morning. They were in town shopping for Kellah's wedding dress.

'I've already spoken to them about our plans,' Kellah said patiently. 'And if you'll give me a minute, I tell you as well. We're getting married at Karingal.'

'Jude's place?' Jilly's voice rose in surprise. 'But Will and I wanted to throw the reception at *our* place.'

Kellah silently gritted her teeth. Much more of this and she'd convince Jude they had to elope. 'Jilly, I'm deeply touched and thank Will for me, please. But this is Jude's and my wedding,' she pointed out gently. 'We want to have it at Karingal. The name means "happy home" so it couldn't be more fitting, could it?'

Jilly gave in gracefully. Grinning, she leaned across and pressed her sister's hand. 'That sounds so *you*, Kel.' And then her hand went to her throat. 'Oh, lord, I just realised I kind of plunged in and assumed you'd want me for your matron of honour. Did you have someone else in mind?'

'You goose!' Kellah clicked her tongue. 'We promised we'd be each other's bridesmaids when I was thirteen and you were eleven—remember?'

'So we did.' Jilly looked wistful. 'It was the day you left for boarding school.'

'Don't remind me.' Kellah chuckled. 'We thought we'd never see each other again.'

'I'm really happy for you, Kel.'

'Thanks.' Kellah looked dreamily into space. 'I'm happy for me, too.'

'OK, finish your coffee.' Jilly was briskly back to business. 'We haven't tried McClintock's yet or that new boutique in the mall—Wedding Fever.'

Kellah's mouth turned down at the corners. 'I haven't seen anything I liked yet.'

'Well, I've really good vibes we're going to find the perfect dress.' Jilly was suddenly full of purpose. 'And with a bit of luck, we might find something half-decent for me to wear as well.'

They went to the new bridal shop first. 'This stuff is so expensive,' Kellah whispered, riffling through yet another rack of gowns.

'Not all of it. What about this?' Jilly held up a slim-line dress of embossed satin, sleeveless with just the suggestion of a train.

'Not bad,' Kellah said thoughtfully.

'You'd need to wear long gloves, though.'

'Forget it.' Kellah shook her head. 'Gloves are a menace.'

Jilly put the dress back and pulled out another. She giggled and held it up. 'This?'

'Please. I'd look like a serving wench.'

'If I might make a suggestion, ladies,' the boutique manager said helpfully. 'I've a bridal gown that arrived only yesterday. I haven't had a chance to bring it through to the showroom yet. You're the bride, I take it?' She looked at Kellah with a warm smile.

'Yes.'

'Then I think this gown might be just what you're looking for. Like to try it on?'

'It'll probably cost the earth,' Kellah fretted as they went through to the fitting room and she slipped out of her denim skirt and pale blue jumper.

Jilly rolled her eyes. 'Stop worrying. Dad's given us a blank cheque. He'll want you to have the best.'

When the manager had settled the gown over her hips and fastened all the pearl buttons up the back, Kellah couldn't wait to look.

'Kel, it's stunning…' Jilly's voice hushed in awe.

'It is, isn't it?' Kellah's face was wreathed in smiles as she paraded in front of the wall of mirrors.

The gown was slim-line in off-white delustred satin, strapless with a beaded bodice, the fishtail design of the skirt creating a little flare around her ankles and at the back.

'There's a matching organza jacket that goes with it,' the manager said now. 'Actually, it's more of a bolero. And it has long sleeves, too.'

Kellah stopped her little twirl and stared in the mirror. 'It's not too…?' She fingered the gown's faint cleavage.

'Don't dare change a thing!' Jilly was adamant. She grinned wickedly. 'Those buttons are rather strategically placed, aren't they? I'll bet your groom will find them interesting.'

Kellah blushed and showed her sister the tip of her tongue.

'There's a tiara that's included as well.' The manager disappeared through the rear curtains and then popped back. She held up the delicate headpiece for Kellah's inspection. 'Some of our brides are opting not to wear a veil these days. Are you wearing your hair up or down?'

'Up,' Jilly said firmly.

Kellah hesitated. 'Jude likes it down.'

'A compromise, then.' Jilly took charge. In a few deft strokes, she'd pulled the combs from Kellah's hair and swept it back from her ears into a fall at the back. Then she coaxed a long tendril down to create a softening effect over one cheekbone. 'Now, try it.' Jilly stepped aside and the manager settled the tiara gently into position.

'Oh, yes…' Jilly steepled her fingers under her chin, a goofy grin on her face. 'It's the absolute finishing touch. We'll take the whole package. Kel?'

Kellah nodded, too overcome to speak. Was that really her in the mirror? she wondered.

Jude's bride.

Her throat lumped. Did anyone deserve to be this happy…?

'I'll have this boxed for you,' the manager said, as Kellah stepped carefully out of the gown. 'And we have a delivery service.'

'If you don't mind, I'd like to take it with me.' Now she'd found her dream wedding gown, Kellah wasn't about to let it out of her sight.

Then the manager asked, 'What about bridesmaids?'

'My sister is my only attendant.' Kellah wound a hug around Jilly's shoulders. 'We're looking for something special for her to wear as well.'

'Let me think, now.' The manager paused for a second. 'You're quite different personalities, aren't you?'

'I'm the bossy one.' Jilly laughed. 'I love primary colours, if that helps?'

'I may have just the thing.' The manager disappeared through the curtains again and returned with a pure silk concoction that had both sisters swooning in delight.

It was a chilli-red two-piece, comprising a strapless, sequined bustier and knee-length skirt. Jilly slid into the stunning outfit as though it had been made for her. She looked across at Kellah. 'What do you think?'

Kellah gave a throaty chuckle. 'You're gorgeous and you know it. Will's eyes will be out on stalks.'

'Should be an interesting night, then.' Jilly chuckled and did a model-like little strut. 'I'll need something for my throat, I think.'

'A lozenge?' Kellah quipped. 'Leave it with me,' she dismissed. 'Jude and I will find you something special. Now we've got the dresses, we should probably decide on our flowers, Jill.'

Jilly did a final twirl. 'Tulips,' she said without hesitation. 'White with touches of deep pink. We'll have identical bouquets. All right with you?'

Smiling, Kellah palmed a shrug. 'You're the artist in the family.'

Kellah took her dress home and hung it carefully from a high point in the second bedroom. And each day she took a peek at the beautiful gown as if to reassure herself that she and Jude were actually going to be married.

Everything came together perfectly. They even managed to get a decent locum to cover the time they'd be away on their honeymoon. *A week from Saturday, I'll be Jude's wife*, she thought, a soft smile playing about her lips as she slid her car into a parking space at the shopping centre.

Slinging her tote bag over her shoulder, she got out of the car, locked it and proceeded to make her way through to the top end of the mall. It was Thursday late-night shopping and she was making her way to the jeweller's.

'Kellah! Wait up!'

Kellah turned expectantly. 'Sarah!' She smiled at Jude's sister. 'Fancy running into you. What are you doing here?'

They walked into the jeweller's together. 'I'm just picking up a couple of rings I've left for resizing. You?'

'Collecting the necklace Jude and I bought for Jilly for being our matron of honour. It's a gorgeous silver filigree design.' Kellah steered Sarah towards the counter. 'Like to see it?'

'Love to.'

Minutes later, with their smart little carry bags dangling from their fingers, the two left the jewellery store together.

'Got time for a coffee?' Sarah asked. 'Or are you on call or something?'

'Free as a bird.' Kellah laughed.

'Let's go in here, then,' Sarah urged, her eyes drawn like magnets to the display of cakes and pastries in the window of a nearby coffee-shop. 'This'll all end up on my hips,' she predicted ruefully a short while later, forking up another mouthful of the lemon meringue pie they'd ordered.

Kellah gave a snip of laughter. 'And I'll probably need safety pins because the buttons won't do up on my wedding dress.'

'I'm so glad you've chosen the late afternoon for your wedding,' Sarah approved. 'It'll be so-o romantic afterwards with the candlelight and everything. Were you happy with the cake lady I suggested?'

'She couldn't have been more helpful,' Kellah said enthusiastically. 'We're going all modern and having a chocolate curl and raspberry layer cake.'

Sarah groaned. 'I can't possibly miss that! I'll have to fast all day.'

Kellah blotted her mouth daintily. 'Everything's come together so beautifully. Sometimes I feel I should pinch myself to make sure I'm not dreaming.'

'My brother's on cloud nine, too,' Sarah said softly. 'And the news that things are finally moving for Kamal's adoption after all this time has placed the seal on his happiness.' She chuckled. 'Would you believe he actually asked me to read the letter from the agency in case he'd got it wrong?'

Adoption? Letter? The words spun round and round in Kellah's head, stabbing painfully like knives. Her stomach turned over, her fingers whitening with the pressure of gripping the handle of her coffee-cup.

What was happening here? Was Jude's proposal of marriage just a way of getting permission to adopt the child at long last? The child he'd been going to rear with Angela?

Dear God.

She went cold. Was he using her merely to satisfy the requirements of the adoption agency? She went colder still, recalling how he'd pushed for an early wedding date…

'Are you all right?' Two little frown lines jumped between Sarah's brows. 'Oh, lord, me and my big mouth. You don't know anything about this, do you?' She clattered her cup back on its saucer. 'Please tell me Jude's told you about Kamal.'

'Yes.' Kellah's throat felt like sandpaper as she swallowed. 'He's told me about Kamal.' He'd just omitted to tell her she was about to become the boy's adoptive-mother—whether she liked it or not.

CHAPTER THIRTEEN

KELLAH hardly knew how she'd got home, remembering only that she'd offered some lame excuse to Sarah and bolted from the coffee-shop.

Her first instinct had been to confront Jude until she'd remembered he had a consult at the hospital. Instead, she'd dropped her head on the steering-wheel and waited for the pain to come.

It hadn't taken long for the tentacles to claw their way around her heart and squeeze. What a gullible fool she'd been. 'Or perhaps I'm just a rotten judge of men,' she'd whispered despairingly.

Back in her apartment, she wandered around like a lost soul. She felt so cold, her heart cut in two. *I trusted you, Jude,* she agonised silently. *Trusted you, listened to you, absorbed your pain into my own body. And what did you give me in return?*

The sudden shrill of the doorbell made her jump. As though her legs belonged to someone else, she made her way along the hallway. Half-heartedly, she opened the door. And froze. 'I can't talk to you, now, Jude.' She made to slam it again but he was too quick for her.

He strode past her into the lounge, turning to address her almost before the door was closed. 'Sarah called me,' he began tightly.

'I might have known you'd stick together.'

'What's that supposed to mean?'

Kellah gave a bitter laugh. 'Your sister blabbed, Jude. I know all about your little secret now. Only it's not so little, is it? I would've thought the adoption of a child is a matter of huge importance. When were you going to tell me?'

His mouth compressed. 'After we were married. Kellah, don't look at me like that. I didn't think it was anything you needed to know beforehand.'

'*Nothing I needed to know?* How could you even begin to think that, Jude? Didn't you imagine I might have wanted some input?'

'Frankly, no, I didn't.' He seemed genuinely puzzled. 'But I see now I should've said something.'

'And isn't *that* the understatement of the year!'

'All right!' Jude's emotions began to show. 'Let's talk about it now!'

'Why bother?' Kellah's mouth trembled. 'I can't marry you, Jude.'

He swore softly. 'For crying out loud, Kellah, you're blowing this up out of all proportion. OK—I made a mistake. I should've told you what was happening with Kamal. I'm sorry.'

Kellah buffeted another wave of anger and disbelief. 'And that's supposed to make it all right, is it? I'm supposed to marry you, become adoptive mother to a child I've never even met, so you can fulfil some kind of—of *fantasy*!'

There was a deathly hush. Jude's face went chalk white and he went on staring at her for a long time, until realisation dawned in his eyes. 'Oh, Kel...' he said unsteadily. 'You've got it all wrong.'

'What?' she demanded. 'Just tell me what I've got wrong.'

'*Everything!*' With a little shake of his head, he muttered something about meddling sisters. 'Kellah, *I* haven't applied to adopt Kamal—but someone else has.'

'S-someone else?'

'Yes,' he confirmed, adding with a faint smile, 'A couple from New Zealand. Drew and Sharon Murdoch. They've been care workers in Qandahar for the past year and spending their free time at the orphanage. They met Kamal.' He swallowed and took a deep breath. 'From all accounts, the little guy just wound his magic around their hearts.'

Kellah's mouth opened and closed. She felt as if she were on a roller-coaster, plummeting towards the ground. Her mind was reeling—and yet a tiny throb of happiness was starting at the back of her head.

'Oh, Jude, could you hold me, please?'

In two steps he'd covered the distance between them, wrapping her in against him. 'Kellah, I'd never deceive you. Not about anything. You have to believe that.'

'I thought you were just marrying me to get Kamal,' she said brokenly. 'You pushed so hard for an early wedding date.'

He clicked his tongue. 'But that was only because I wanted us to be together. I hadn't even opened the letter from the adoption agency when I asked you to marry me.'

'You hadn't?'

'No. They'd written to me care of Sarah's address. She'd brought it into the surgery that day we went out to see Alby Nissel—the day I asked you to marry me.' He eased away and looked down at her with a brilliant smile.

'Oh, lord, I remember now.' Kellah closed her eyes and turned her head, tears spilling down over her cheeks. Lifting her hands, she scrubbed them impatiently away. 'You even mentioned your mail and I asked you if you wanted to open it.'

'And if I remember rightly, I said I'd get to it later. Oh, my love, don't cry. I should have explained what was happening. But I thought I'd burdened you enough with my past.'

'And I should have talked to you, instead of jumping to all those conclusions. And flinging all those terrible accusations at you.'

'Can we forget any of this ever happened?' he said deeply. 'My ghosts have all been laid to rest, thanks to you. You, Kellah Beaumont, are the woman I love. I want to be with you for the rest of our lives.'

She looked up into his eyes, swamped by the look of love she saw there. 'We'll make lovely memories of our own,' she whispered, swallowing the huge lump in her throat.

'And lovely children,' he murmured against her lips. 'I adore you.' His voice shook with the strength of his emotions.

'Oh, Jude, forgive me for doubting you…' Her voice broke and she buried her face in his shirt.

Beneath her cheek his chest heaved, and his arms tightened around her, crushing her against him.

'Enough, now,' he whispered, easing her away. And then his lips were on hers in a kiss of the sweetest kind, a kiss that was so long and so tender that all the uncertainty and pain were banished.

'Did you feel any kind of regret when you found out Kamal was going to another family?' Kellah snuggled closer to Jude on the sofa.

'A little tug perhaps,' he admitted. 'But I'm pleased for him. And his adoptive parents would have been thoroughly screened so I have no worries on that score. The agency people were just doing me the courtesy of telling me what had been decided and that there was no need to send any more money.'

Kellah hid a smile. 'But we will, of course.'

He turned his head so he could look at her and his eyes had never seemed so blue. 'Did you say *we*?'

'Yes.' She toyed with the top button on his shirt. 'Perhaps I could get to meet this young man some day? What do you think?'

Jude kissed the tip of her nose. 'I think that could be arranged. New Zealand's only a few hours' flying time away. I've already had a very warm email from Drew and Sharon inviting me to visit. But, of course, I'll be taking my wife now, won't I?'

She blinked and took a shaken breath. 'I thought I'd have to take my beautiful wedding dress back.'

'Sweetheart.' His thumb stroked her cheek, brushing away the tiny stray tear. 'That was never going to happen. I can't wait to see you as my bride.'

Kellah felt her eyes prickle again but a radiant smile lit her face. *Jude's bride.* They were just two tiny words.

But they meant everything in the world.

Your opinion is important to us!

Please take a few moments to share your thoughts with us about Mills & Boon® and Silhouette® books. Your comments will ensure that we continue to deliver books you love to read.

> To thank you for your input, everyone who replies will be entered into a prize draw to win a year's supply of their favourite series books*.

1. There are several different series under the Mills & Boon and Silhouette brands. Please tick the box that most accurately represents your reading habit for each series.

Series	Currently Read (have read within last three months)	Used to Read (but do not read currently)	Do Not Read
Mills & Boon			
Modern Romance™	❏	❏	❏
Sensual Romance™	❏	❏	❏
Blaze™	❏	❏	❏
Tender Romance™	❏	❏	❏
Medical Romance™	❏	❏	❏
Historical Romance™	❏	❏	❏
Silhouette			
Special Edition™	❏	❏	❏
Superromance™	❏	❏	❏
Desire™	❏	❏	❏
Sensation™	❏	❏	❏
Intrigue™	❏	❏	❏

2. Where did you buy this book?

From a supermarket ❏   Through our Reader Service™ ❏
From a bookshop ❏   If so please give us your Club Subscription no.
On the Internet ❏

Other _____   _____/_____

3. Please indicate by number which were the 3 most important factors that made you buy this book. (1 = most important).

The picture on the cover ___   I enjoy this series ___
The author ___   The price ___
The title ___   I borrowed/was given this book ___
The description on the back cover ___   Part of a mini-series ___

Other _____

4. How many Mills & Boon and /or Silhouette books do you buy at one time?

I buy ___ books at one time ❏
I rarely buy a book (less than once a year) ❏

5. How often do you shop for any Mills & Boon and/or Silhouette books?

One or more times a month ❏   A few times per year ❏
Once every 2-3 months ❏   Never ❏

6. How long have you been reading Mills & Boon® and/or Silhouette®?
_____ years

7. What other types of book do you enjoy reading?

Family sagas eg. Maeve Binchy ❏
Classics eg. Jane Austen ❏
Historical sagas eg. Josephine Cox ❏
Crime/Thrillers eg. John Grisham ❏
Romance eg. Danielle Steel ❏
Science Fiction/Fantasy eg. JRR Tolkien ❏
Contemporary Women's fiction eg. Marian Keyes ❏

8. Do you agree with the following statements about Mills & Boon? Please tick the appropriate boxes.

	Strongly agree	Tend to agree	Neither agree nor disagree	Tend to disagree	Strongly disagree
Mills & Boon offers great value for money.	❏	❏	❏	❏	❏
With Mills & Boon I can always find the right type of story to suit my mood.	❏	❏	❏	❏	❏
I read Mills & Boon books because they offer me an entertaining escape from everyday life.	❏	❏	❏	❏	❏
Mills & Boon stories have improved or stayed the same standard over the time I have been reading them.	❏	❏	❏	❏	❏

9. Which age bracket do you belong to? Your answers will remain confidential.

❏ 16-24   ❏ 25-34   ❏ 35-49   ❏ 50-64   ❏ 65+

THANK YOU for taking the time to tell us what you think! If you would like to be entered into the **FREE prize draw** to win a year's supply of your favourite series books, please enter your name and address below.

Name: _____
Address: _____
_____
Post Code: _____ Tel: _____

Please send your completed questionnaire to the address below:

READER SURVEY, PO Box 676, Richmond, Surrey, TW9 1WU.

0904/03a

MILLS & BOON®

Live the emotion

_Medical
romance™

DOCTOR AND PROTECTOR *by Meredith Webber*

(Police Surgeons)

Dr Cassie Carew can't believe the mysterious letters
she's received are significant. But the police bring in
surgeon turned criminologist Dr Henry McCall to
protect her. And he's posing as her lover! Cassie has to
cope with a threat to her life and a flood of medical
emergencies—but it's her unwanted bodyguard who's
always on her mind!

DIAGNOSIS: AMNESIA *by Lucy Clark*

When GP Logan Hargraves was called out to an
unconscious patient he was amazed to find medical
researcher Dr Charlotte Summerfield. Why was she
alone in the Outback? Had she come to see him, after
their first electric meeting? Logan was hoping for
answers—but Charli woke with amnesia…

THE REGISTRAR'S CONVENIENT WIFE
by Kate Hardy

(A&E Drama)

Single dad Eliot Slater is worried he might lose custody
of his son. Could a marriage of convenience help him?
Consultant paediatrician Claire Thurman is good friends
with Eliot, her registrar, and is secretly rather attracted
to him. But when he asks her to be his convenient wife,
she discovers it's not enough. She wants him for real!

On sale 1st October 2004

*Available at most branches of WHSmith, Tesco, ASDA, Martins,
Borders, Eason, Sainsbury's and all good paperback bookshops.*

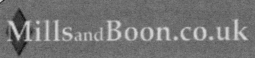

FREE!

4 Books
and a surprise gift!

We would like to take this opportunity to thank you for reading this Mills & Boon® book by offering you the chance to take FOUR more specially selected titles from the Medical Romance™ series absolutely FREE! We're also making this offer to introduce you to the benefits of the Reader Service™—

- ★ FREE home delivery
- ★ FREE gifts and competitions
- ★ FREE monthly Newsletter
- ★ Exclusive Reader Service offers
- ★ Books available before they're in the shops

Accepting these FREE books and gift places you under no obligation to buy, you may cancel at any time, even after receiving your free shipment. Simply complete your details below and return the entire page to the address below. You don't even need a stamp!

YES! Please send me 4 free Medical Romance books and a surprise gift. I understand that unless you hear from me, I will receive 6 superb new titles every month for just £2.69 each, postage and packing free. I am under no obligation to purchase any books and may cancel my subscription at any time. The free books and gift will be mine to keep in any case.

M4ZEF

Ms/Mrs/Miss/Mr ....Initials................................
BLOCK CAPITALS PLEASE
Surname ....
Address..

....

....Postcode ....

Send this whole page to:
UK: FREEPOST CN81, Croydon, CR9 3WZ